CROWN COURT
Killer

DAHLIA DONOVAN

HOT TREE PUBLISHING

MARINE | THE BOTANIST | THE UNEXPECTED SANTA |
THE LION TAMER | HAKA EVER AFTER

For information, contact the publisher, Hot Tree Publishing.

www.hottreepublishing.com

Editing: Hot Tree Editing

Cover Designer: BooksSmith Design

E-book ISBN: 978-1-922679-19-2

Paperback ISBN: 978-1-922679-20-8

To my betas, for keeping me going when I wanted to give up on this story.

ONE

OSIAN

"A MASSIVE THANKS TO OUR SPECIAL GUEST— solicitor extraordinaire Wayne Dankworth, whose insights into criminal litigation have been fascinating. As always, I'm Osian Garey. My partner in crime is Dannel Ortea." Osian winked at his husband-to-be, who simply rolled his eyes. "Hope you've enjoyed this week's episode of our London Crime Podcast. Don't forget to tune in next time. This has been Oz and D. Signing out."

Dannel waited until Osian hit pause to let out a loud groan. "And you'd done so brilliantly right until the end."

When Osian looked at Dannel, he was always reminded of Richard Ayoade, if the actor were taller, buffer, and a retired firefighter. Whereas Osian felt like a washed-up version of the actor who'd played Constantine on the telly, less buff, shorter, and scruffier.

"Nothing wrong with Oz and D," Osian insisted. They had this debate at least once every podcast. He got up to stretch, having sat for several hours getting their recording together. "I'm knackered."

"Are you still not sleeping well?" Wayne paused in sifting through the papers he'd brought to glance at Osian in concern.

"Nightmares aren't conducive to a good night's rest." Osian believed healing started with being open with his friends and family. "My therapist thinks being trapped in the well aggravated my post-traumatic stress."

A former paramedic, Osian had resigned after losing a patient through no fault of his own. He'd spent over a year trying to unpack the trauma left behind. His recovery had taken a hit three months ago.

While trying to solve a murder, Osian had come face-to-face with the killer. He'd been forced into an old well along with their elderly neighbour, Ian Barrett. Rescue had eventually arrived.

His nightmares had begun not long after. Dannel often sat up with him, and they'd play video games or listen to a cast album of whatever musical had grabbed their attention until he was too exhausted to remain awake.

Thanks to the lack of sleep, Osian felt a hundred years old and not thirty. His therapist did help. It would simply take time.

He fully intended to avoid old wells in the future.

And killers.

And fake ghosts haunting theatres masquerading as killers.

"Are you joining us for coffee and footie in the morning?" Wayne went back to packing up the files. "Chelsea versus Tottenham. Clash of the titans."

Wayne was shacked up with Dannel's younger brother, Roland. The latter had moved into the former's swanky flat. They had a larger telly, so Dannel and Osian occasionally went over to watch their rival Premier League football teams do battle on the pitch.

"Of course." Osian nodded. Dannel readily agreed as well.

"Bugger." Wayne checked his phone when it beeped, muttering a few additional curses under his breath. "I've got to go."

3

"Problem?" Osian followed him to the door, watching him drag on his overcoat.

"Barnaby being Barnaby." Wayne rushed out the door, shouting a "goodbye" halfway down the stairs.

"Who's Barnaby?" Osian wondered. He closed the door when it became clear Wayne had already made it out of their building in record time.

"A barrister." Dannel had begun packing up their microphones. "Rolly mentioned Wayne had quite a dust-up in Crown Court with the man."

"Did they throw their wigs?" Osian always found the court accoutrements to be entertaining. "Swirl their robes around dramatically?"

"Words were exchanged." Dannel snorted in amusement at Osian as he waved his hands around. "They were chastised by one of the judges. Not sure Wayne wears a wig. Isn't that just for barristers?"

"We'll ask Wayne tomorrow to give us the juicy details."

"Or we could mind our own business?"

"In the face of potentially interesting court gossip?" Osian went over to help Dannel clean up. They'd recently exchanged their small kitchen table for a larger one more conducive to the equipment needed for their weekly podcast. "Did you see the email from Archie?"

"About the new love of his life?"

"Let's hope this one's less prone to extortion and murder." Osian didn't think their old friend had the best of luck when it came to romance.

Three months ago, Archie had been faced with the murder of his mother. His love interest had been inexplicably intertwined in the case and wound up dead as well. They'd only just come out of it alive after Osian's close call in the well; Archie had fled to his beloved backpacking as soon as the police cleared him and arrested the killer.

Osian couldn't blame him for wanting to leave. Their LGBTQ+ First Responder Coalition did miss Archie, though. They'd all been a founding member of the support group for former and current paramedics, police officers, and firefighters. His best friend, Abra, and Dannel's best mate, Evie, led the organisation currently.

"Mum wants to chat about the wedding plans." Dannel brought up the subject they'd been avoiding for the last week. "I have slight regrets."

"About proposing?"

"About telling everyone else I proposed." Dannel packed the last of their recording gear into the hall cupboard. "We don't have to make a whole meal of the wedding."

Osian didn't necessarily disagree, but their mums had opinions on the matter. "What if we turn control over to Olivia?"

"Would she mind?"

"Would she mind planning our wedding? Have you met my baby sister?"

"Yes. We grew up next door. I've known Olivia her entire life." Dannel hopped up onto the kitchen counter, watching Osian get the kettle going. "You were being rhetorical."

"I was." Osian dug through one of the cabinets, hunting for their box of tea. Dannel, as an autistic, occasionally had trouble deciphering when someone was facetious, sarcastic, or rhetorical. "How are we out of tea?"

"You made the last shopping list," he pointed out helpfully. "Suppose we could run by the supermarket."

"Maybe pick up cinnamon buns and mochas at Nordic Bakery on the way?" Osian had yet to meet a pastry he didn't love. "I'll text Olivia to see if she wants to take on the circus that our mums want to turn the wedding into, yeah?"

"Princess Olivia to the rescue."

"She could rule the world." Osian lived in awe of his younger sibling. He also thought she had experience corralling the madness of their family when it came to weddings. She was happily married to her beloved Drystan Rees, an overly cheery Welsh firefighter who used to work with Dannel. "I doubt she'll say no."

"She can't resist throwing a party." Dannel switched off the kettle. "I'll grab my wallet. Coffee is calling my name."

"Cake is calling both our names. Something to keep us going while we start the new armour project." Osian was excited. They'd been commissioned to create a full cosplay set based on one of the designs for the character Hawke from the second *Dragon Age* game. His personal favourite. "Get my keys and wallet as well, please?"

Moving over to the kitchen window, Osian stared out at their colourful corner of Covent Garden. They lived in an exciting hub that made the heart of London. *Maybe I'm a bit biased.*

Since they'd both retired from emergency services, they'd focused on building their podcast and cosplay fabrication business. Osian hadn't imagined a career other than as a paramedic. And yet, they were thriving.

Thriving.

Such a millennial word.

Yet, here we are, thriving.

Aside from the occasional murderer.

He did wonder if it might be easier and simpler to live in a quieter place. They'd have more time for building their businesses—maybe. Dannel might find life less stressful without the crowds and chaos of London.

"Ready?"

Osian was jerked out of his thoughts. He turned to find Dannel fighting with the knot on his trainer laces. "Do you ever wish we moved away from London? Live somewhere in the country, maybe?"

"No." Dannel's response was immediate and emphatic. "Leave London? I love it here. Why?"

"No reason."

He gave his shoelaces one last frustrated yank. "Weird question to ask out of the blue. Is this a neurotypical thing?"

Osian went over to take the trainer out of Dannel's hand. "How do you bungle up a knot this badly?"

"Just cut the laces. I've got a spare set some-where," Dannel grumbled impatiently. "Inside voice?"

"Close enough."

Over the years since Dannel's official autism

diagnosis, he'd learned to rely on others to help him not shout or whisper. He struggled to modulate his voice. Osian knew it greatly frustrated him.

Osian struggled with the knot before tossing the trainer back to Dannel. "Buggered those up, didn't you? Have you superglued your laces?"

"Tired of the sodding things coming undone while I'm in the gym. I've only narrowly avoided tripping. These laces hate me. Grab the scissors, will you?"

After a bit of creative cursing and a quick snip, Dannel freed his trainers. He put in the new laces. Osian chuckled when he beamed the old ones into the bin with enough force to almost knock it over.

"You showed them."

Dannel stood by the door and inhaled deeply, closing his eyes for several seconds. "Okay. Let's get fuel for the rest of the day."

"Is cake fuel?"

"It's usually enough of a fuel to get us motivated, if only to find more." He made an excellent point. "Are you coming?"

The cake wound up being a selection of almond twists, apple Tosca buns, and chocolate-orange croissants. They bought enough to share with their neighbours, Adelle and Stanley, who lived downstairs with their Yorkie, Thames. The couple frequently brought treats for them; it was only fair to return the favour.

Their vibrant three-storey apartment building had been around since the fifties. His uncle and aunt owned it along with the shop on the ground floor and rented out the flats. They all had a close relationship with their neighbours.

In retrospect, it was likely one of the reasons Dannel would never consider moving. He was comfortable. Their flat and neighbours were home.

Why even consider leaving his safe space?

With enough sugar and coffee to have them buzzing, the two got down to the business of creating a set of armour. They pulled screenshots from the game. Dannel began sketching out the various pieces required.

He had a deft hand at design. Osian barely managed a straight line with a ruler. His main job in the early stages involved checking through their inventory for supplies.

Dannel sat up when his phone beeped jauntily. He shook his hand out to relax his fingers, then grabbed it, peering at the screen. "Rolly."

"What's Constable Rolo want?" Osian snickered along with Dannel.

They enjoyed teasing the youngest out of their quartet. They'd all grown up together, since their mums had lived across the hall from one another. Osian and Dannel had been best friends basically from birth and in love from the time they'd known what it meant.

"Apparently, this barrister Barnaby shouted at Wayne in the middle of the office, called him an amateur." Dannel seemed as surprised as Osian. "Never met anyone as dedicated to their clients as Wayne."

"I imagine he's not going to take being dressed down in public well." Osian knew he'd have been irate if a co-worker had yelled at him like a naughty child. "Poor Wayne."

TWO

DANNEL

"It's too early." Dannel launched his pillow at the clock across the room. They'd placed it on a shelf out of easy reach to keep them from snoozing the alarm constantly. "It's not even daylight yet."

"We've got to be up in time to watch Chelsea smash Tottenham." Osian rolled away from Dannel when he tried to shove him off the bed. "Don't be jealous. My team's success isn't a direct reflection on you."

"Please stop talking utter twaddle." Dannel repeated the last word a few times. It had a satisfying rhythm. "We promised to bring part of breakfast over to watch the game with Rolly and Wayne."

"It's not twaddle when my team's higher up the

table than yours." Osian needled him further. They'd supported rival London football teams from the time they were kids. "Would you rather not watch?"

Dragging himself out of bed, Dannel chose to ignore his fiancé. It would only encourage him to keep talking nonsense. There was no way his team would lose.

The only time Osian and Dannel ever disagreed on anything was over footie and which bread made the best toasties. A promising sign, in his mind, to the strength of their relationship. His parents had argued over loads of things until they'd divorced.

Dannel put that thought out of his mind; he didn't want to think about his dad's push for reconciliation. He was trying to be less stubborn. It wasn't easy for him, no matter how much everyone encouraged him.

He didn't understand how non-autistics seemed to easily forgive and forget.

Maybe twenty-plus years is too long to hold a grudge when I didn't understand what was happening at the time to begin with?

Maybe.

Does any kid grasp the intricacies of their parents' relationship?

Probably not.

During the journey to Wayne's flat, Dannel mulled things over. His proposal to Osian had forced the issue with his father. If they had a full-on wedding, Myron would obviously want to be there for his son.

Or so Dannel had been told by everyone else in his family.

The jury was still out for him.

"We're here." Osian nudged him out of his thoughts. "Not sure the Uber driver wants to idle forever."

"Sorry." Dannel muttered an apology to the driver and got out of the car. He leaned his forehead against Osian's shoulder after the vehicle had driven away. "Maybe we should've stopped for coffee."

"Poor lad." Osian reached up to gently massage Dannel's neck. "It could always be worse."

"How?"

"Chelsea could've already won."

"Arse." Dannel went to push him away when flashing lights caught his attention. "Ossie."

"Hmm?" Osian followed his gaze to the numerous police vehicles blocking off a section of the car park. "Someone's died."

"Checked your crystal ball?"

"Don't be daft." Osian gestured to a group off to

one side near the entrance to the building. They walked closer, trying to see what was happening. "Haider's over there. Why else would they call him in, since he mostly handles homicides?"

"Rolly." Dannel spotted his brother speaking with Detective Inspector Haider Khan. Roland was waving his hands about quite animatedly. "He's not happy."

"Inside voice," Osian murmured. "Let's not draw the attention of the nice constables and detectives just yet."

"Look." Dannel elbowed Osian in the side, nodding his head toward a familiar figure seated in the back of one of the police vehicles. "Not good."

"Wayne locked up in the back is more than not good." He caught Dannel by the arm, guiding him forward. "Let's see if Haider will tell us anything."

"Wayne's car."

They'd moved close enough to easily see the vehicle cordoned off with caution tape. Several detectives were inspecting the interior while others, who Dannel recognised from the coroner's office, lifted a body out of the boot onto a stretcher. He had a sinking feeling in the pit of his stomach.

"Danny." Roland drew their attention, jogging

over. He gripped Dannel's arms tightly as if he'd fall over without the hold. "They won't listen to me."

Gone was his confident and strong brother. Dannel awkwardly hugged Roland. He couldn't recall ever seeing him so affected.

Dannel didn't quite know how to help his brother. He couldn't tell if Roland was angry or sad; deciphering emotions didn't come easily to him. "Who's not listening to you about what?"

"DI Khan. Any of them." Roland shook his head, stepping back and standing up straight. "They've taken Wayne in for questioning because they found Barnaby's body in his boot."

"I'd honestly hoped we'd run out of dead bodies to find." Dannel kept a hand on his brother's shoulder.

"Maybe third time's the charm?" Osian suggested.

"We've discovered more than three bodies." Dannel noticed several of the detectives continuing to inspect Wayne's vehicle. "What have the police found?"

Maybe if they focused on the facts, Roland would have a chance to collect himself. Dannel would do anything to help his little brother. He also didn't believe Wayne was capable of murdering anyone.

Destroying with sharp words? Definitely. Wayne had a gift with them. It made him a devastating opponent to face in court.

"Constable Ortea. I see you've found support-ers." Detective Inspector Khan joined the three of them. "Why are you two always at my crime scenes?"

"We can't always be at your crime scenes," Dannel argued. "Not logical. You've had more than three cases in the months we've been acquainted. If you haven't, London's got a lower crime rate and a higher number of detective inspectors than I imagined."

"He didn't mean literally every crime scene." Osian leaned in closely, keeping his voice low.

"Right." Dannel appreciated Osian's always keeping an eye or ear out for him, helping him when things got muddled up. "Have you arrested Wayne?"

When in doubt, distract them with a difficult question.

"We haven't made any arrests," Haider insisted. "A body has been found in the boot of his vehicle. The death was clearly not accidental. We quite naturally have questions needing to be answered. Mr Dankworth has thus far refused to cooperate."

"Asking for his solicitor to be present isn't a lack of cooperation." Roland folded his arms across his chest. He glowered at Haider, who remained unmoved. "He's within his rights to not speak with the police."

"I agree." Haider nodded. "We can't, however, ignore the facts. Once we have him at the station and his solicitor arrives, I'm sure we'll get to the bottom of things quickly."

"We could—" Osian started only to be cut off by Haider immediately holding a hand up.

"You could both stay out of this. Haven't you come close enough to serious injury playing amateur detective?" Haider glanced behind him when one of the constables called his name. "I'll try to keep you up-to-date with what's happening."

They watched him stride across the car park. He got into the vehicle with Wayne and drove off moments later; Roland muttered several curses under his breath. It had definitely not been the best way to start their day.

Dannel grabbed his brother when he went jogging towards his car. "Where you going?"

"I'm not leaving Wayne to face a potential

murder charge on his own." Roland tried to jerk away from him. "Let go, Danny."

"Focus. Who's Wayne's solicitor?" Osian leapt into the conversation. "Get them on the phone. They'll want to know what's happened and be there with Wayne. We'll hang around here for a few minutes to see if we can't sniff out any of the details."

"I'm going," Roland reiterated. He had his phone out and was already beginning to dial. "Give me a second. Not sure I should drive."

"Of course you shouldn't." Dannel had no doubts his brother would stand firmly behind Wayne. "Just remember to try not to give them a reason to sack you."

Despite his constant protesting about not being a detective yet, Dannel knew his brother had ambitions for his career as a police officer. Roland putting himself out for Wayne might tank those goals. Not that it mattered to him.

"What would you do for Osian?"

Dannel didn't need to consider the what-if. Osian had been falsely accused of murder several months ago. "I'd do anything I possibly could."

"Exactly," Roland muttered through gritted teeth. "And so would I."

THREE

OSIAN

WHEN THE POLICE DROVE OFF WITH WAYNE, Osian had worried he'd have to restrain both Ortea brothers. He hadn't been looking forward to the attempt, but they'd calmed themselves down. A small miracle.

It didn't take long for Roland to disappear. One of the barristers from Wayne's firm showed up. They'd be representing him during the police interrogation.

Once Roland had left, Osian turned his attention to Dannel. They'd both been hoping for a calm November. And no more bodies. Hadn't three murders in a row at the Evelyn Lavelle theatre been sufficient?

"I see Willa." Dannel pointed toward a well-dressed woman chatting on her phone near the entrance to Wayne's building. "I think. Maybe?"

Wrapping his arm around Dannel's shoulder, Osian eyed the woman. She did seem familiar. He knew Dannel often struggled with remembering faces.

It had become almost a phobia.

"Why don't we go have a chat with her?" Osian thought it might be helpful to get an outside perspective on what happened before they arrived. Roland had been too upset to give them any information. "Or you could snoop around Wayne's car while I speak to her?"

"Excellent plan. I'll be sneaky."

"Just pretend you're walking around on the phone. No one ever pays attention when someone's nattering to someone." Osian gave Dannel a quick kiss then made his way over to the solicitor. She finished up her conversation as he walked up to her. "Willa Abraham, right?"

She eyed him suspiciously for a moment before accepting the hand he'd held out to her. "Obsidian? Right?"

"Osian." He tried not to laugh at her obvious dismissal of his existence. "We met at one of Wayne Dankworth's parties. You work with him, right?"

Willa raised an eyebrow at him. She didn't answer for several moments. "Oh, yes, you're the one who pretends to be Sherlock Holmes."

Pretends?

Bit rude.

If anything, Dannel and I bumble along while everyone else assumes we're investigating.

That's my story, and I am sticking to it.

Osian decided to harness her disdain into something more useful. "Police seem to be drawing a lot of attention this morning."

"They found a body in the boot of Dankworth's car." Willa was suddenly almost gleeful in her excitement. She'd definitely been waiting to share what she knew with someone. "Not surprised."

"Oh?" Osian tried to appear only mildly interested. She might clam up if he pressed too hard. "Was he acting suspiciously?"

"Hadn't you heard? Barnaby Sharrow, he's the one in the boot." Willa shifted closer when one of the detectives went by. "He cocked something up in court, hurting one of Wayne's clients in the process. They had a fantastic argument, got themselves into trouble with a judge."

"Did they?"

Willa nodded. "I wasn't surprised."

"At the argument?" Osian prompted when she fell silent.

"About Barnaby. He's annoyed a fair number of people at the firm. Drinking in the office, leaving files about. He's shown up late for court. I even heard from another barrister he punched a judge. No idea why they didn't arrest him." Willa sniffed dismissively. "No one knows what's going on with him. Or *was*, I suppose."

"You don't seem beaten about his death." Osian made a mental note to find more out about the judge.

"Barnaby jeopardised one of my cases recently. I'd been preparing to make a complaint about him." Willa shrugged. She checked her phone when it beeped. "Dankworth's saved me the trouble of dealing with the forms."

"You said he punched a judge?" Osian couldn't help his curiosity.

"Judge Hamnet Allsop. He's an old crony of Barnaby's wife and her family. Old money. You know the type." Willa held her phone up. "Must take this."

Walking away without another word, Willa returned to the building. Osian decided to add her name to the suspect list. And the judge. He hadn't wanted to pepper her with too many questions initially.

He joined Dannel, who'd found a bench not far from Wayne's vehicle. One of the constables appeared to be preparing it to be towed. They probably had to take the car somewhere more secure for processing.

"Find out anything interesting?" Osian leaned into Dannel, who had his phone in camera mode, focused on the police. "Clever. We can review the video at home."

"Apparently, Wayne and Roland called the police." Dannel pocketed his phone when one of the constables glanced in their direction. "They came out to get something from his car and found...."

"A stiff?"

"Ossie." Dannel shushed him. "But yes, basically. They called the police. Constables obviously detained Wayne since the car belongs to him. Detectives arrived. How does a body get into someone else's vehicle?"

"Happens in movies all the time when someone's being framed."

"This isn't a movie." Dannel fell silent when the constable glanced in their direction again. "Inside voice?"

"Not quite." Osian coughed through a laugh. He didn't want to draw any more attention to themselves. "Why don't we go to the police station? Offer moral support."

"Pretty sure Haider will call it offering to be a distraction and disruption." Dannel stood up and grabbed his phone. "Uber?"

"Why don't we walk? We can pop by a coffee shop. I'm going to need more than what we've had to handle yet another murder mystery." Osian decided leaving sooner rather than later would be wise. The constable kept looking over at them. "Ready?"

Making a quick getaway, they strode away from the car park. Osian found it hard to fathom anyone believing Wayne capable of murder. A man wholly dedicated to truth and helping others. He went so far as to offer his services free of charge to those in need.

Wayne? Murder someone? Not a chance.

So, the question is, who wants the police to believe he did it?

Barnaby Sharrow's body had definitely been placed in Wayne's boot on purpose. The killer didn't pick a car randomly. They'd obviously attempted to get rid of two solicitor birds with one murderous stone.

"I've got a few potential suspects." Osian waited

until they got far enough away from the police to speak.

"Already?"

"Willa, definitely. A judge. And Barnaby's wife."

"His wife?" Dannel paused to wait at the zebra crossing.

"It's almost always the spouse." Osian had done loads of research for an upcoming podcast episode all about the subject. "Or maybe not every time, but enough to make them top on the list of potential suspects."

After picking up coffee at the café around the corner, they made their way to the Charing Cross police station. Osian wasn't sure what they'd accomplish. He wanted to be there for Wayne, nevertheless.

Coffee in hand, they walked up the steps toward the police station. Osian had a strange sense of déjà vu. He remembered the immense anxiety from being questioned about his friend's death.

Questioned by Haider and several other detective inspectors.

Suspected of murdering her when Osian had, in fact, been attempting to save her life. It had been Wayne who'd come to the rescue, talking his way around the detectives. He'd met their probing questions with pointed logic.

Osian believed in returning favours. He wasn't sure they were clever enough when it came to the law to be as much help as Wayne had been. "Ready to storm the castle?"

"More of a building than a castle." Dannel paused on the top step.

"Castle's a building, isn't it?" Osian opened the door for him, bowing slightly. "After you. Beauty before the Beast."

"Daft git." Dannel kept his voice low. "What if they don't let us in?"

Osian didn't get a chance to answer. He spotted Detective Inspector Khan waiting for them inside the lobby. "Expecting us?"

"One of my constables spotted you on the way here." Haider seemed almost resigned to their presence. "Mr Dankworth is speaking with his solicitor at the moment."

"Is he?" Osian pressed his lips together to keep from grinning at the obviously irritated detective. "You'd miss us if we weren't here. How else would you solve your homicide cases?"

"Forensics? Witness statements? CCTV footage? Mobile phone messages and tracking?"

Haider ticked the items off on his fingers. "The list is endless."

"I mean, don't hold back. Tell us how you really feel. We're devastated by your casual dismissal." Osian struggled not to snicker when he heard Dannel's surprised laugh that he managed to turn into a coughing fit. "See? He's all choked up by your disregard of our talents."

"I'm sure." Haider motioned for them to follow him. He led them through the door off the side of the reception area and back to his office. "Have a seat."

"I sense a lecture coming." Dannel perched on the edge of a chair, obviously prepared to bolt if necessary. He was the very picture of unease.

Osian sat beside him, reaching a hand out to rest on his arm in the hopes of calming him down. "DI Khan knows we're harmless."

"Harmless menaces who stumble into dangerous situations under the guise of solving mysteries." Haider glanced pointedly between the two of them. "I'm hoping to head you off this time before you embroil yourself in my murder investigation."

"Wayne's not a killer," Dannel blurted out. "He's not."

"We haven't accused him of anything—"

"Yet." Osian cut the detective inspector off mid-sentence. "You had him sitting in the back of a police car and dragged him here for interrogation."

"First, stop watching detective shows. It makes you overdramatic." Haider held a hand up to stop them both from reacting. "Second, we found a body in the boot of his car. What else could we possibly do but bring him in to answer a few questions? He's not been arrested. We haven't accused him of anything. Third, have you considered the possibility that if he's innocent, someone's obviously after him? Fourth, and most importantly, you are not investigators."

"Bit harsh." Osian didn't think they'd done so badly in the past, even if identifying the killer had been more accidental than intentional. "We're not completely useless."

Haider pinched the bridge of his nose, shoving his glasses up and sighing so deeply that Osian wondered if it came from the depths of his soul. "Please don't make my case more complicated than necessary."

"Have a little faith." Osian tried to appear contrite. He wasn't sure he succeeded. "Can we see Wayne?"

"I'm sure he'll be thrilled to see you once we've finished." Haider answered a call on his phone, stepping outside for privacy.

Osian watched the detective speak animatedly on the phone. "How do you sneak a body into the boot of a car without damaging the boot?"

"No idea." Dannel shrugged. "They went out last night. Maybe they stole Wayne's keys, killed Barnaby and shoved him in the boot..."

"And returned the keys without anyone the wiser?" Osian had to admit stranger things had happened. "It's not the most implausible crime we've ever heard of."

Haider stepped back into his office, slipping his phone into his pocket. "As much as I enjoy bantering with you two, I'm going to have someone escort you outside. I can't have you hanging about while I speak with Mr Dankworth."

"Haider?" Osian felt a knot in the pit of his stomach.

"Trust me to do my job." He gestured toward the constable now standing by the door. "I'm sure Constable Ortea or Mr Dankworth will speak with you soon."

"I trust you," Osian admitted.

It's everyone else who's anxious to close a case without actually solving the crime that I don't trust.

FOUR

DANNEL

"DON'T THE POLICE USUALLY ESCORT PEOPLE into the station and not out the door?" Dannel had waited for the constable to return to the building before commenting. "What exactly did Haider think we'd do if left alone in his office?"

"Rummage through his files for information?" Osian sat on one of the brick walls on either side of the steps. "Why don't I text Roland? He's probably not in the interrogation room. He might be able to fill us in on what's happening."

Sitting on the wall opposite him, Dannel tried not to notice the constable keeping an eye on them from inside the station. He pulled out his own phone. A little research would help make the time pass by more quickly.

What was the victim's name again?

Barry Shallow?

No. Bugger. Why am I always so pants at remembering names and faces?

"Barnaby Sharrow." He cringed and lowered his voice immediately. *One day I'll be able to not shout everything. It'll be brilliant.* Osian caught his attention, obviously interested in what he'd found. He read off from the Adam Street Chambers website. "Barnaby Sharrow. Defence Barrister. Experienced in difficult and sensitive cases. A talented courtroom advocate dedicated to working with you and your solicitor to advance your case."

"Quite the CV. Was he a junior barrister, or had he progressed to Queen's Counsel?"

"He's not taken the silk yet," Dannel recalled the term Wayne often used for those who'd been appointed to the respected role. "His wife works on the clerk's team at the Adam Street Chambers."

"Does she?" Osian came over to sit beside him. "Maybe she caught him having an affair."

An affair was definitely a motive. They'd discussed so many crimes on their podcast involving one partner killing the other over cheating. She was definitely on the top of his list of suspects.

He figured the police would be investigating her.

They had to be. If nothing else, Haider tended to be incredibly thorough in solving his cases.

"Or he caught her." Dannel continued perusing the website. "They've defended a number of high-profile characters based on the cases they list."

"Defence barristers usually do. Everyone deserves good representation, whether guilty or not." Osian motioned for him to click on one of the links. "Any names amongst the barristers stand out?"

"Not really." Dannel scrolled through the long list of barristers. "I wonder if Barnaby lost anyone else's case like he did for Wayne's clients."

A quick internet search brought up several articles about Barnaby, including one about his death. Dannel skimmed each one. He dismissed most of them as useless.

"Willa claimed the judge was an old friend of Judie Sharrow née Astley." Osian had his phone out as well. "Hamnet Allsop. Let's see what we can find out about him. Well, he looks like someone straight out of one of Ian's plays."

Hamnet Allsop looked exactly like his name sounded to Dannel. A member of the wealthy upper crust of society, friends with members of parliament and other dignitaries. He'd gone to all the right schools, knew all the right people, and had a country estate to retreat to in the summer as if they were still living in Edwardian times.

"I imagine boarding school wasn't a walk in the park with a name like Hamnet." Dannel did an internet search cross-referencing the judge's name with Barnaby Sharrow. "Interesting. Loads of articles about him in connection with the Astley family."

"What about Sharrow?"

"Not much. Most of the articles mention Judie Astley." Dannel clicked on an article with a family name. "Solicitor Willa Abraham and her client Satish Misra blame Barrister Barnaby Sharrow for the loss of his suit against his employer. Mr Misra claims Sharrow mishandled evidence in his case, costing him potentially millions."

Osian glanced up from reading the article along with Dannel. "Here we go."

Dannel followed his gaze to find Roland, Wayne, and his solicitor coming out of the station. "Finally."

"Have you two been giving the detectives a hard time?" Wayne gave them both a tired smile. He leaned into Roland, who had an arm around him. "I could do with something to eat. Sorry, you've missed your game."

"Sod the game." Osian jumped off the wall.

"Why don't we pick something up and head over to our flat? It's comfortable and private."

"Both equally important." Dannel teetered on the edge of being overstimulated from the stress and chaos of the morning. He hated when their schedule changed rapidly without warning. "Why don't we swing by Pizza Pilgrims? Grab enough for the five of us if your solicitor wants to join us."

"Bradley Nichols, life saver. Meet Roland's brother, Dannel, and his tag along, Osian Garey." Wayne peered behind him at the police station. "Shall we? You're more than welcome to join us, Nichols, unless you've work to be done."

"On a weekend? I'm supposed to be enjoying a bit of rest and relaxation." Bradley didn't bat an eyelid when Osian shook his hand, but Dannel simply waved. "Since I've the only vehicle, why don't I give everyone a lift? Just point me in the right direction."

After a bit of conferring, Roland headed to Wayne's flat to keep an eye on the police presence there. He made them promise to keep him informed. Dannel could see the worry on his brother's face.

Who could blame him?

Bradley Nichols reminded Dannel of a solicitor from a show on the telly. He had the gravity of one.

Like he'd burst into a rousing speech at any second to win his case.

While they made their way to Pizza Pilgrims, Dannel stared out the window. He was dying to know what had happened in Wayne's conversation with detectives. Had they given him any details?

Anything at all?

Through the drive and picking up pizza, Wayne remained silent. He checked his phone obsessively. Dannel was content to let Osian and Bradley chat.

There was nothing wrong with a bit of silence.

Nothing.

When they arrived home, Dannel remembered to check the score of the game. He'd completely forgotten. Their teams tied.

Brilliant.

Chelsea nil, Tottenham nil.

Well, at least Ossie can't lord it over me that his team won or has jumped up the table.

After setting the box in his hand on the coffee table, Dannel fled to the bedroom. He sat on the mattress and took a moment to centre his mind. *Ossie can handle things for a few minutes. He's better at small talk with strangers.* "What an absolutely bizarre turn of events."

FIVE

OSIAN

"Everything all right there?" Wayne asked after Dannel had disappeared.

"Perfectly fine. He'll be back when he's ready. So, what the bloody hell happened with you?" Osian went into the kitchen to pick up a stack of mismatched plates, then handed them to Wayne and grabbed a case of fizzy drinks from the refrigerator. He carried the box into the living room, where Bradley had arranged the pizza. "Well?"

"I should probably be warning you off getting involved." Wayne slid several slices of pizza onto a plate and immediately took a bite. "We got up early this morning to pick up breakfast before the game. Wait, no. I should start the story with last night."

After having a few bites, Wayne went through

their night out with a group of fellow attorneys. He'd briefly revisited his argument with Barnaby Sharrow. But after intervention from Willa, they'd put their disagreement to bed.

"What's the difference between a solicitor and a barrister?" Dannel came over to sit beside Osian, picking up a slice of pizza. "I can never remember."

"We're both attorneys. Barristers tend to specialise in certain areas of the law. They're often brought in on complicated cases to handle matters in court." Bradley spoke up from where he'd been quietly enjoying his pizza. "Solicitors are usually the ones to bring them into a case if it's going to trial. Laws are changing, though. Clients can now hire barristers directly."

"Right." Dannel nodded a few times. Osian had a feeling Bradley's explanation hadn't been concise enough for him to process. "Okay."

Note to self, try to explain to Dannel later. It'll bother him for days, otherwise. Lawyers always use too many words when two or three would do.

"So, let me get this straight. You got sozzled on a night out." Osian wondered how their vehicle had gotten to the flat. He knew neither Roland nor Wayne would've driven under the influence. "How'd you get home?"

"Willa Abraham went with us since we live in the same building. She hadn't planned on drinking, so she became our designated driver." Wayne rubbed his forehead, trying to think back. "My memory's a little fuzzy. I had to pick up my keys from her flat this morning."

"Did you?" Osian remembered his brief conversation with her at the crime scene. "Willa Abraham had control of your car and keys. During the night when someone slipped a body into the boot?"

"Yes." Wayne reached for his last slice of pizza. He set it down after a second without taking a bite. "And I'm sure she's about to become highly annoyed with me, since I've pointed the police in her direction."

"Wait. Hang on." Osian remembered his conversation with Willa earlier. "She claimed you and Barnaby were still angry with one another. Why? You said she mediated between you. She never mentioned it, going so far as to claim Barnaby had ticked her off as well."

"Did she?" Wayne sat forward in the chair. "Odd."

Suspicious. Not odd.

Or maybe equally odd and suspicious behaviour.

"She said Barnaby had been drinking in the

41

office." Osian wondered how much of what Willa had claimed was true. "Did he punch a judge?"

"I saw the punch," Bradley commented. "We both did. They'd sniped at each other for most of the trial. It was unusual."

Wayne nodded his agreement. "Never saw Barnaby drink in the office—or out of it, for that matter. I believe he was teetotal."

"He was teetotal. His family are Quakers." Bradley reached out to grab a second slice of pizza. "He wouldn't touch the stuff, not even at his wedding. Willa lied."

"Why?" Dannel asked the question on Osian's mind. "What's her motivation to lie about him? Especially to Ossie."

"She joked about us being amateur detectives," Osian remembered. He'd found the comment strange. "Maybe she wanted to throw me off the scent?"

It didn't make sense. There were too many gaps in their knowledge. Osian didn't envy Haider trying to solve the case.

The obvious option would be to arrest Wayne. If rumours of his fight with Barnaby had been spread far and wide, it offered an attractive motive to the detective. The body was found in Wayne's vehicle, after all.

All incredibly convenient.

Too much so.

"So, who wanted to get rid of both Wayne and Barnaby?" Dannel broke the silence that had followed Osian's rhetorical question. "Kill one and frame the other for it. They didn't randomly select a stranger's car. They picked Wayne, got the key, hid the body, and managed to return the key."

"We've either got a skilled car thief and murderer, or Willa was involved. How else would they get the key?" Osian considered the options for a moment. "The killer might've stolen it from her."

"Seems a terribly large amount of work for one murder. Why go to the hassle?" Bradley spoke while scrolling through something on his phone. "I've asked one of our clerks to keep an eye on Willa for the day."

"It's a massive amount of work for one murder," Wayne agreed. "I've handled enough criminal defence to know the path of least resistance is the one most villains use."

"And we're back to Dannel's point of who wanted to target you as well as Barnaby." Osian leaned back into the sofa, resting his feet on the coffee table. "Did you have many cases in common?"

"A few. We'd only lost one of them." Wayne scratched his jaw, lost in thought for a few seconds. "We had one angry client and one angry judge in common."

The suspect list didn't offer Osian a massive amount of hope. A judge, a solicitor, a wife, and a client. None of them were likely to volunteer much information to the police, let alone to him or Dannel. He wondered if they could tag along with Wayne to his office.

It might be too obvious of a tactic. They didn't know anyone involved in the court aside from Wayne. As a paramedic, his work life didn't often bring him in close contact with the crown court.

"What next?" Dannel poked Osian in the side after everyone had been quiet for a reasonably long time. "Are we just going to sit around to wait for something to happen?"

"Neither of us do sitting around and waiting well. We get bored too easily." Osian glanced over at the two attorneys who were glued to their phones. "Something wrong?"

"Willa's been questioned by the detectives. She's going on a rampage in our office group chat." Wayne answered while Bradley typed away on his iPhone. "Claims I've set her up for murder. How have I set anyone up when the body was in the boot of my car? Does no one stop to think?"

If they do, they might seriously think you've done it.

Osian didn't think his initial thought would be helpful to anyone. "They've obviously let her go without arresting her if she's having a go at you."

"What an absolute mess," Wayne groaned. He dropped his phone on the coffee table and slumped back into his chair. "She's telling everyone I'm trying to frame her for murder."

"She had your car keys all night," Dannel pointed out. "How could you frame her for murder when she controlled access to your vehicle?"

"That is the point I will make to the police when they ask, since I'm sure she pointed them right back at me." Wayne reached a hand up to massage his forehead. "We should head into the office. I want to nip this in the bud if I can."

"Threaten them with murder." Osian grinned when Wayne glared at him. "Trying to lighten the mood."

"Not sure you're helping." Dannel nudged him

with his elbow. "Aren't you supposed to meet with Abra this afternoon?"

Osian glanced at his watch. The day had flown by so far. "Haider might be investigating my murder if I don't leave soon."

"Why don't we give you a lift?" Wayne offered.

Rushing to the bedroom, Osian quickly changed into more comfortable clothes. He'd promised to go for a walk with Abra. They weren't as dedicated to staying fit as Dannel and his best friend. A walk was definitely more their speed.

"Doesn't Abs have an aunt or uncle who's a judge?" Dannel had followed him to the bedroom, likely not wanting to be forced to make small talk.

"I think it's her godmum, maybe. She calls her auntie, though. I'll ask." Osian kicked himself for forgetting. Abra might be able to get them background on Hamnet Allsop. "Can we call the judge 'Hamster'?"

"No."

"You are a ruiner of fun."

"First, not a word. Second, not true. Third, calling a judge Hamster would be fun in the short-term and detrimental to our lives in the long-term." Dannel dodged the socks Osian threw at him.

"Point. Made."

Dannel snickered with him. "Go on. You don't want to make the solicitors wait too long."

Osian finished dragging a hoodie over his T-shirt. He slipped over to wrap his arms around Dannel and gave him a quick snog. "Love you."

SIX

DANNEL

With the flat to himself, Dannel turned on the *Hamilton* cast album. He cleaned up the living room and kitchen while singing his heart out. It helped him clear his head.

Checking the calendar in the kitchen, Dannel realised they'd missed their day to sweep the stairs. He grabbed the broom in the corner. His uncle relied on them to help keep things tidy.

With the door open, Dannel could continue listening to music while sweeping their floor. He was grateful for neighbours who didn't mind a bit of *Hamilton* and being in a small building. Two floors with a single flat on either side made cleaning up an easier task than a place like Wayne's.

"Hello, duckie."

Dannel peered down the stairs to find Adelle and Stanley waving up at him with their little Yorkie bouncing around their feet. "Off for Thames's afternoon walk?"

"Are you boys still coming to the dinner in a few days?" Adelle asked. It was the couple's turn to host their building meal this time around. They all took turns. "We've gone with a Greek theme this time around. I did mention to Ian that a toga was allowed if he promised to bring something other than red wine."

"Greeks didn't wear togas. They wore himations. Which did kind of look like bed sheets, to be fair." Dannel couldn't help grinning when Stanley winked at him. "Ossie and I can pick up baklava if you like."

"Don't worry about sweeping up our floor. I did it yesterday." She waved before heading down the stairs.

Shaking his head, Dannel finished up their floor. Adelle and Stanley were a lovely retired couple in their sixties who'd lived in the building for as long as he could remember. They'd been the ones to come up with the idea of having a dinner party.

They'd been having them for years now.

Everyone attended. They alternated the host and theme each time.

It had brought all of them closer. Ian tended to throw the most extravagant ones. He was the true definition of eccentric, often sashaying around in a luxurious dressing gown.

His toga would probably be made from the most expensive silk. Ian had lived a fascinating life. In his eighties, nothing seemed to be slowing him down, not even his close call with death a few months prior.

I want to be like Ian when I grow up. Maybe less boisterous and extroverted. And I'm not sure I can pull off his charismatic personality.

No one could possibly be as charmingly extroverted as Ian. The man was a force unto himself. Dannel gathered up his little pile of dust and jogged down the stairs to reach the ground floor entryway.

"Hello, darling." Ian opened his front door with a flourish, his dressing gown draped around him. "Fancy a cup of coffee?"

Dannel leaned against the top of the broom handle. "Not really. Thanks."

"Having a quiet day then? Hold on just a moment, darling." Ian held a hand up before disappearing into his flat, then reappearing moments later with a box. "My lovely assistant brought lemon drizzle buns for me. I couldn't possibly eat all of them. Here. Share them with your dreamy fiancé."

Saying a quick thanks and goodbye, Dannel trudged upstairs to their flat. He held the broom under one arm with the box of treats in his other. It required a bit of juggling to get inside and lock the door behind him.

Will Ossie mind if I enjoy all of these by myself? He'll never know if I do. Is true love sharing treats when he doesn't even know we have them?

True love is definitely the sacrifice of sugary treats.

I should make tea. And have a bun. And clean the kitchen.

His mind kept throwing out tasks to accomplish. Dannel closed his eyes, trying to slow himself down. It occasionally felt as though his brain were a carousel careening into warp speed.

He was still staring at the box in his hands when the doorbell rang. He almost dropped the precious package in surprise. "Sodding sod it."

Taking a few seconds to still his suddenly racing heart, Dannel went over to the door. He took a few more deep breathes. *I am not up for dealing with conversation right now.*

"Hello." Myron stood with his hand raised to knock on the door when it opened. "Son?"

Dannel clutched the box in his hands, glowering at his father's nose. "I need you to not add more noise right now."

"Bad day?" Myron hesitated before stepping into the flat. "I can come by later. Do you need me to call Osian?"

Progress?

Maybe he can learn.

Of all the members of his family, his father had been the one who hadn't approved of his relationship with Osian. His mum always claimed it was a personality conflict. Dannel never understood what she meant. He wasn't the one dating Osian, after all. What did it matter if their personalities clashed? How did that even work?

"I'm fine."

"So fine, you're crushing the box?" Myron didn't sound convinced. "You're obviously not wanting to have a chat with anyone right now. I'll come by later."

To his surprise, Myron immediately turned and left the flat. Dannel stared at the closed door. He didn't know what to do with himself; standing in the middle of the room wasn't accomplishing anything.

Sitting on the sofa with the box of buns still in his head, Dannel had a massive headache brewing. He tilted his head back to rest against the cushion. Today was not his day.

"Dannel?"

He opened his eyes, peering up at Osian, who had gently shaken his shoulder. "What time is it?"

"Late afternoon. Your dad messaged me to suggest I give you some space." Osian sat on the arm of the sofa. "I thought he was trying to get me to cancel the wedding at first. Instead, he was worried I might disrupt your much-needed quiet."

"Odd." Dannel scrubbed his fingers across his face, trying to wake himself up. "I expected him to push, but he left me in peace."

"Maybe, just maybe, he's trying to show you how serious he is about reconnecting." Osian reached a hand out to help him sit up. "Did you have lunch? I brought pasta from my lunch date with Abs."

"Did you find anything interesting out?" Dannel stood up, stretching and batting away Osian's hand when he touched his exposed abdomen where his shirt rode up. "Ossie? About the judge?"

"Abs is going check in with her godmum. She did say Hamnet Allsop had a reputation amongst the clerks at the court for philandering ways and wandering hands." Osian handed over the container of leftovers he'd brought. "A brilliant discovery if we were looking for his killer. There's no end of suspects."

"Unless the judge killed him to keep his secrets safe?" Dannel carried what appeared to be a massive piece of lasagne into the kitchen. "We know there was animosity between them."

After reheating the lasagne, Dannel grabbed two forks and returned to the sofa. He offered one to Osian. It saved having to fend off him stealing food, despite him already having eaten with his best friend.

Osian twisted around to lie down and ignored the fork. "Go on. I'm sure you're half starved."

Dannel settled back on the sofa. "Can you message Rolly for me? See how Wayne's doing. I don't think I'm up for conversations with anyone at the moment."

Aside from Ossie.

"Have you ever wanted a pet?" Osian asked. He shuffled down the sofa until his head rested on Dannel's thigh. "And don't say you have me."

"You're a person, Ossie. Not a pet." Dannel grabbed the remote and started flipping channels on the telly. "We can't even keep a plant alive."

"We haven't really tried."

"We killed Olivia's prize orchid when we plant-sat for a week. A week." Dannel settled on a sport channel showing a recap of the football matches. He tossed the remote onto the coffee table. "Who murders a plant in seven days?"

SEVEN

OSIAN

A FAINT ELECTRONIC TUNE BROUGHT OSIAN OUT of the deepest sleep. He tried to figure out why the Comic-Con announcer suddenly sounded like his phone. His eyes refused to open.

Sleep was good.

"Your phone." Dannel elbowed him in the side.

Osian threw his arm, trying to locate the annoying sound without opening his eyes. He knocked over everything on the nightstand in the process, including the lamp and a bottle of water. "Bugger."

"Your. Phone." Dannel gave him a harder shove, then dragged a pillow over his head. "Make it stop."

With immense effort, Osian rolled out of the covers. He fumbled around on the floor. His phone continued to go off incessantly until he fished it out from under the bed.

Osian sat up, leaning against the bed to see who wanted to speak with him at seven in the morning. "Of course."

"Problem?" Dannel's muffled voice came from underneath the pillow.

"Not sure. Go back to sleep." Osian rubbed his eyes to clear them. *What on earth does Roland want at this time of day?*

Roland: Wayne's been brought in for questioning again.

Osian: In handcuffs? Or all friendly like?

Roland: They were very insistent. Not friendly but not hostile either. I've already called Bradley. Just wanted you to know. Don't tell Dannel. He'll only worry about me and Wayne. I'm heading to the station.

Right.

Well, we don't keep secrets from each other so how am I supposed to keep this a secret?

"Problem?"

Osian glanced up and found Dannel leaning

58

over the edge of the bed. "Fancy a walk to the police station?"

"Wayne?" Dannel sat up immediately and made to stand up. He stopped when Osian looped an arm around his legs. "What? We should go. Rolly must be so worried."

"He's a copper."

"And? It doesn't mean he won't be worried about Wayne. He's in love." Dannel reached down to drag his fingers through Osian's hair. "Aren't we supposed to provide moral support?"

Yes, but I wasn't supposed to tell you.

"Yes, I suppose we should. Wayne's certainly done that and more for us." Osian didn't think Haider would appreciate the pressure of having so many people present. "I wonder if the police have their warrant for Wayne's flat. It might explain the additional questions."

"Rolly didn't want you to tell me." Dannel made an accurate and educated guess. "You'd think he was the older brother. I can handle bad things happening without falling apart."

"Hence why we won't share any doughnuts with him." Osian got to his feet, already formulating a plan. "We might have time for a shower if we share."

"We take longer together than we do individually." Dannel didn't argue and followed him into the bathroom. "Why are we getting doughnuts?"

"You don't think Detective Inspector Khan would appreciate a snack?"

"Let's try not to make things more difficult for Wayne and his solicitor." Dannel shook his head at Osian when he grinned.

"The solicitor's solicitor."

Showering together did take longer, but they thoroughly enjoyed it. Dannel threw on clothes quickly, disappearing out of the bedroom. He hated the sound Osian's hair made when he combed it.

How does my hair even make a sound? Despite Dannel's insisting his hair made a clicky sound, Osian had never heard it. He didn't argue.

Just because I can't hear the sound doesn't mean it's not there.

And Dannel certainly had better hearing than he did.

"Safe yet?" Dannel poked his head back into the room. "How long does it take to comb your hair? It's short."

Osian tossed the comb onto the bed. "I'm done. Doughnuts await us."

"And our friend potentially going to jail for a murder he didn't commit."

"Well, yes, but nothing seems quite so bad with a mouthful of sugary sweetness." Osian didn't mind poking at the detectives a little. He still held a little resentment for being accused of murdering one of his good friends. "You ready?"

By the time they'd gotten dressed and ready, their Uber had arrived. They had the driver take them in one direction to pick up the pastries, then back to the police station. Coffee and doughnuts made the extra bit worth it.

"You brought doughnuts." Roland stared, disbelieving, at the box Osian held out for him. "This isn't some barmy American sitcom."

"Not hungry? Will it mess with your street cred?" Osian teased while keeping an eye out for Dannel. He didn't often process the subtle variations of annoyance well, and Roland's voice had definitely gone up a notch. "We got your favourite from Doughnut Time. If you're not—"

Roland snatched the doughnut out of the box, glaring at him and taking a bite. "Thanks."

"Right. Teasing," Dannel muttered.

They found a quiet corner out of hearing of the front desk to chat. Roland kept glancing toward the closed door leading further into the station. He obviously hoped to see Wayne and his solicitor.

"What happened?" Dannel asked after his brother finished the doughnut. "Why've they brought him in again?"

"They wouldn't tell me anything. Dragged Wayne off for questioning." Roland waved them closer, keeping his voice low. "One of the DIs not on the case happens to be a mate of mine. She told me they've found the murder weapon."

"And?" Osian prompted when Roland fell silent.

"A tie."

"A tie?" Dannel sounded as confused as Osian. "Why would they bring Wayne in for a tie?"

"The tie was Wayne's. He wore it in the office the day of the murder. Several people saw him, including a few police officers who happened to be in court." Roland rubbed his eyes tiredly. He gratefully accepted the coffee Dannel handed to him. "Cheers. I know Wayne didn't murder anyone. But the evidence is a killer."

"Pun intended?" Osian knew they faced an uphill battle with the growing evidence against Wayne. "Have they arrested him?"

"Haider claimed they only wanted to ask a few more questions." Roland gestured wildly, sloshing coffee over his clothes. "Damn it. I've got to be on duty in an hour. How am I supposed to focus with this looming over us?"

"Why don't you head out? Get yourself changed and ready. We'll stay here and keep vigil over the interrogation." Osian didn't need to glance at Dannel to know he was nodding his agreement. "Getting yourself in trouble won't help Wayne. He's in good hands with his solicitor."

And you drawing attention to yourself won't do much good either.

The detectives might decide to poke into Roland's life as well. He and Wayne were dating, after all. Who else would they assume had helped him commit murder?

"They won't let us into our flat," Roland admitted. "I'm sure they're going over it with a fine-toothed comb."

"Why don't you come to our place? You can find something to wear there." Dannel patted his brother awkwardly on the back. "I'll go with you. Ossie can stay here. He's better at chatting with the police than I am."

"You do brilliantly." Osian rushed to assure him. Dannel always handled things better than he thought. "We should message Chris."

"Why?" Roland glanced anxiously over when

the door opened only to sigh when it was someone else being escorted by a uniformed officer. "How's he going to help?"

"Mr James Bond? He might have contacts." Osian was mostly teasing. He did think their well-connected security expert friend might be able to dig up something about the case or the people involved. "It never hurts to have help."

After a bit of back and forth, Roland and Dannel left together. Osian let them take the leftover dough-nuts. He'd had enough of them and didn't need to inhale the entire box on his own.

Using his phone, Osian spent an hour reading and responding to emails to their podcast account. They'd asked listeners to send in their true crime stories for them to share in an upcoming episode. One from Cornwall had proven particularly intriguing.

Who finds a body in the garden of their newly inherited cottage?

The sender also happened to be autistic. Osian couldn't wait to share the email with Dannel. Maybe she'd be interested in being on their podcast to tell her story directly.

"Why am I not surprised?" Haider interrupted Osian in the middle of responding to one of the emails. "Why are you loitering at the police station?"

"Where else can I eat doughnuts and respond to emails?" Osian hit send on the last message and put his phone away. He stretched his arms over his head, trying to appear casually disinterested. "I appear to have misplaced my solicitor. Have you seen him? Taller than me; not as handsome, though. He's a clever bloke. Friendly. Highly unlikely to have strangled someone with one of his expensive ties."

"How..." Haider pinched the bridge of his nose while counting to twenty under his breath. He glowered at Osian, who continued to do a few stretches in the chair. "I don't want to know the details. I'd only have to reprimand someone."

The door opened for a second time, revealing Detective Inspector Powell followed quickly by Bradley Nichols. Osian had a knot in the pit of his stomach. He waited several seconds before realising Wayne wasn't showing up.

"They're holding him." Bradley stated the obvious when he spotted Osian. "For twenty-four hours."

"Right." Osian got to his feet. He glanced over at the detectives, then nodded to Bradley. "Right. You're taking care of him."

"Of course. I've got your number." Bradley seemed to understand the undertone. He stepped between Osian and the two detectives when Haider moved to speak with him. "I'll call you later."

Striding out of the police station, Osian took the steps two at a time. They had a mystery to solve. He refused to allow Wayne to be dragged under by someone obviously intent on ruining his life while getting away with murder.

Once outside, Osian messaged Chris and several of their friends. He wanted to make sure they had all the help possible. Wayne had saved him from a similar fate, after all.

Pocketing his phone, Osian noticed a Rolls-Royce Phantom parked across the street. It was definitely a chauffeured vehicle. The slightly tinted windows kept him from getting an eye on the passenger in the back.

"Osian?"

He glanced behind him to find Bradley walking down the steps. "I thought you were going to call me later."

"Technically, it is later." Bradley paused, peering around Osian to stare across the street. "What is he doing here?"

"He? Who?" Osian twisted around to notice the Rolls-Royce suddenly driving off. "You know them?"

"I know the driver." Bradley watched until the vehicle disappeared around a corner. "Belongs to the Allsops. I've seen him arrive at court and at events with his wife."

"Interesting. Why would they be here? Watching the police station." Osian moved the judge up his list of suspects. "Could one of the Allsops be involved?"

"Possibly." Bradley turned back to Osian. "What are you planning?"

"Planning?"

"Wayne told me all about your adventures with solving murders." Bradley motioned for Osian to follow him down the street. "Tube station's not far from here. I've got to head to the court to meet with another client. What are you planning? How can I help?"

"Has Wayne said anything?"

"He's innocent," Bradley immediately retorted.

"Of course he is." Osian rolled his eyes. "He's a clever bloke. He must've considered who might want to set him up to go down for murder."

"We compiled a list yesterday." Bradley rested his briefcase against a wall, then opened it and rifled through the various papers. He handed one to Osian. "I've already made a copy. He said you'd want one."

"Brilliant." Osian took a cursory read of the list. Most were names he'd already thought about. "Who's Edgar Smith?"

"The judge's security officer. They're thick as thieves. Hamnet went to school with Smith's father. He was handpicked for the position. I imagine he feels beholden to him." Bradley closed his briefcase. "I've got to run. Text me if you have any questions about the list."

The list didn't clear anything up for Osian. He still had so many questions. How were they going to help Wayne without answers?

Could they help him?

EIGHT

DANNEL

Despite having prepared himself, Dannel didn't know how to handle the sudden influx of noise in their flat. He kept his focus on Roland, who'd shown up not long after Osian had returned. They were waiting for Abra, Evie, Olivia, and Drystan to arrive with food.

Chris would arrive later. He had work to finish. They'd gotten lucky with the others being on shifts that allowed them to come over for a late lunch.

Roland hadn't been so lucky. He'd arrived at work only to be immediately suspended with pay, pending the murder investigation. Dannel hoped this wouldn't be the end of his brother's career.

It was mid-afternoon when everyone had gathered together over a massive selection of chicken and chips from Nando's. Roland had settled himself in the corner of the living room. Dannel didn't blame him; their flat felt rather cramped at the moment.

"Okay." Osian drew everyone's attention, tapping his knuckles against the coffee table to stop the whispered conversation between his sister and her husband. He'd arrived straight from the station, smelling faintly of smoke. The hazards of being a firefighter. "We've got a crime to investigate."

Dannel was a little surprised to see nods from everyone. He'd expected someone to argue for allowing the police to do their jobs. Roland usually advocated for them to mind their business. "We don't have much of anything to go on."

"Step one is to gather information." Osian made a flourish next to the first item on his notebook. "We have a number of suspects with motives against both Barnaby and Wayne, since we can safely assume they framed him for a reason. Maybe we can, by process of elimination, find the real killer amongst the list."

Abra leaned forward to peer at the list. "I can take the judge. My godmum's sure to have more gossip on him. I might even be able to chat my way into a dinner party or event where he'll be in attendance. She's always complaining about the number of invites she receives each week. Maybe Chris can give me a hand."

"Give who a hand with what?" Chris's head popped up from where he'd been having an intense conversation with Bradley in the kitchen. He glanced over at the wickedly grinning Abra, who repeated herself. "Of course I can. We can chat about it afterwards. I'll walk you home."

"Why don't you two just admit you want to snog each other in a dark corner somewhere? We're all dying of suspense for when you'll finally get over yourselves." Osian easily blocked the chip Abra threw at him. "We've still got a solicitor, a client, and an angry wife or two."

Names were divvied up to everyone except Roland. He'd gone over to speak with Bradley and Chris. Dannel worried about his little brother but didn't know how to help him.

What Roland needed and wanted was Wayne out of jail and the threat to both of their careers over. A tall ask, but they had to try. Dannel would do anything to help his brother.

"How are you doing?" Osian leaned over, resting his head on Dannel's shoulder. "Shall I chase everyone out of the flat? Not much we can do from here. Plus, if they leave, we've got a shed-load of chips to eat by ourselves."

"I'm all right." Dannel didn't particularly enjoy having their small flat filled with people. He'd deal with it to help Roland. "For another hour or so, I think."

The investigative party didn't last another hour. Abra and Chris snuck out early under the pretence of wanting to speak with her godmum. They refused to acknowledge the whistles chasing them down the stairs.

Evie vanished soon after, eager to get some rest after a long shift at the fire station. Wayne's solicitor followed soon after. Dannel thought the poor man looked dead on his feet.

"How are you doing?" Olivia came over to sit next to him on the couch.

"Me? I'm fine." Dannel shrugged.

"Wayne's going to be okay. And so will Rolly." She glanced over to where Roland was chatting with Drystan. "We'll have him stay with us tonight since their flat isn't accessible. What's the point of having a spare room if people don't stay over?"

"Library? Office? Workspace to make costumes?"

"Rhetorical question." Olivia glanced around the living room. "Why don't I give you a hand cleaning up after the herd of goats who've left crumbs everywhere?"

Dannel continued to stare at her, not moving.

"Rolly will be okay."

"Wayne might not be." Dannel stopped her from repeating herself. He wasn't sure the police would look much deeper, given the amount of evidence they'd already found.

Wayne's car.

Wayne's tie.

Wayne's argument in front of witnesses with the victim.

It made for a compelling case against him. Dannel had even had doubts at first. He'd never voice them to Olivia.

And he felt guilty for having the thought.

Unlike Osian, who often believed the best of everyone, Dannel tended to be more practical and suspicious. Given the right motivation, anyone could be driven to kill. *What would I do if someone threatened Ossie in some way?*

"Dannel?" Olivia placed a hand hesitantly on his arm. "You went quite still all of a sudden. Are you okay? Why don't I corral everyone out of the flat so you can have some peace and quiet? We're a rowdy lot at the best of times."

Not wanting to admit to where his mind had gone, Dannel settled for a nod. It would be nice to have the flat to themselves. Plus, he had his eye on the leftover chips and chicken.

In her usual General Olivia manner, she hurried everyone out of the flat. Dannel always found it amusing and intimidating how easily she managed others. She was definitely going to take over the world.

"Chicken, chips, or both?" Osian gathered up the plates, carrying them into the kitchen, then returning to the open packets from Nando's. "There's enough here for an evening snack and probably lunch tomorrow."

Dannel went for the chips, tossing one into his mouth. "Could Wayne have murdered Barnaby?"

"Of course not...." Osian trailed off, considering the question. He flopped back onto the sofa. "No, I can't see him ever being angry enough to kill. Plus, he settled things with Barnaby. Someone's definitely framed him."

"Why?"

Osian grabbed a handful of chips from him. "What if Wayne knows something about the killer?"

"But if Wayne knows who the killer is, why isn't he saying so?"

"What if he doesn't know he knows what the killer thinks he knows?" Osian leaned into Dannel when he sat beside him.

"I have no idea what you said." He raised his hand to stop Osian from repeating himself. "Don't. It's too late in the day for you to break my brain with your explanations."

"Is it late? Sorry." He chuckled, not sounding apologetic at all. "Think the police would let us see Wayne?"

"Don't know why they would. How is it going to help?"

"Maybe we can help jog his memory. See if anything about our list of suspects stands out. Someone's framed him." Osian gave a massive yawn. "We've got to help him figure out why."

It was a long shot.

"You've had worse ideas." Dannel kicked his trainers off and rested his feet on the coffee table. "Why don't we go by the police station in the morning? We can record our podcast in the evening. Are you going to help me fabricate the gauntlets for the Hawke armour?"

"Tomorrow?"

"In between solving murders and recording the podcast." Dannel felt tired thinking about all of it.

"Maybe put the podcast and commission at the top of our list? They pay the bills."

"Yeah, maybe we don't tell Wayne that." Osian grinned at him. "Too practical."

"How can you be too practical?"

NINE
OSIAN

Morning came far too early for Osian the next day. He groaned in complaint when Dannel yanked the blanket off both of them. Not even a warm shower helped coax his mind into functioning.

Dannel guided him out of the bedroom and into the kitchen, gently keeping him from stumbling. "What on earth is going on with you? I haven't seen you this tired since we pulled all-nighters in school."

"I kept tossing and turning last night." Osian dropped into one of the chairs around their kitchen table. "I didn't drift off until around four in the morning."

"Coffee?"

"A mountain of it." Osian dragged his fingers

through his still-damp hair. "Maybe some toast? Or don't we have a few pain au chocolat left?"

"Several flaky pastries with chocolate centres coming up." Dannel bent down to bump his nose against Osian's head, then continued into the kitchen. "How do you make a liquid into a mountain?"

"Freeze it."

While Dannel hunted around to find the leftover croissants, Osian grabbed a scrap of paper and pen from across the table. He wanted to jot down a brief list of what they had to accomplish. *Podcast, gauntlets, visit Wayne, Abra's godmum, chat up neighbours, solve a murder. How hard can that be? Oh, and find time to plan our wedding.*

Dannel came over to set two mugs and plates on the table. He glanced at the list. "We'll never get all of this done. Maybe we should divide and conquer?"

"Sounds like a lot of effort." Osian rested his head on the table, twisting slightly to watch Dannel getting breakfast ready. "Why don't I drag Abra out to pick her godmum's brain for a second time? I can swing by the police station as well. Maybe see if Haider will let me chat with Wayne. You and Roland go by his flat. What if one of the neighbours saw something? They may not have wanted to tell the police."

"Rolly is the police."

"He knows how to tone down the copper." Osian glanced down at the list he'd made. "Podcast can wait until this evening, as can the gauntlets. In fact, we can work on our script while beginning the fabrication."

Dannel brought over the pain au chocolat after heating them briefly in the microwave. "They should release Wayne today."

"Or charge him." Osian was trying to remain hopeful. The evidence had definitely been stacked against their solicitor friend. "They've only got a few hours left before they have to do one or the other."

Over coffee and chocolate croissants, they made their plan of attack for the day. Abra had already texted him to say she was on her way. Dannel had plans to meet his brother at their family shop in an hour.

By the time Abra buzzed the intercom downstairs, Osian had managed to wake up a little more. The coffee and sugar rush had helped. He gave Dannel a quick snog, then rushed downstairs to meet up with his best friend.

"Change of plans." Abra handed him a cup from her favourite café. "I picked up lattes for both of us."

"Are we not meeting your godmum?"

"Auntie Sue's busy in court this morning; however, she's suggested we head over to the Old Bailey. One of her close friends knows Hamnet quite well. They're at the Central Criminal Court today and can show us around." Abra sipped her coffee, then looped her arm around Osian's free one. "The Hamster Judge is presiding over the case. We might get to see him in action."

"If the rumours are true, I'd rather not see him in action." Osian paused before starting across the street with Abra at his side. He tried not to stop in the middle of the road when a vehicle parked nearby caught his attention. "Abs? See the Rolls-Royce?"

"Tinted windows? Definitely something we could never afford to touch, let alone own?"

"The same vehicle was parked across the street from the police station." Osian wondered why a judge's chauffeured Rolls-Royce Phantom kept popping up. "Did you notice someone following you?"

"Me?"

"Maybe our questions drew the hamster's attention?" Osian forced himself not to peer over his shoulder. "Or it's a coincidence. It can't be the only Rolls-Royce Phantom in London."

"They'd go out of business if it was." Abra glanced behind them, ignoring his admonishment not to look. "Car hasn't moved."

"You'd make a terrible spy."

"I'm a paramedic." She shrugged. "Come on. I don't want to be late."

Putting aside his unease, Osian picked up the pace and definitely didn't peer over his shoulder every five seconds to check for the Rolls. They arrived at the Old Bailey in good time. The Central Criminal Court loomed large in front of them.

"Is your godmum's friend one of the clerks or a barrister?" Osian kept to one side to avoid being crushed by the bustling throng inside the newer of the two buildings that made up the court. He hadn't had much need to spend time in a court that tended to handle the worst criminal cases. "I'm definitely underdressed for the occasion. Even the people queued up to get seats in the public gallery are better prepared than I am."

"This is what happens when you dress yourself," Abra snarked. She eyed his jeans and favourite N7 T-shirt. "Honestly. A T-shirt in court?"

"Just representing my people."

"Mass Effect players aren't your people." Abra motioned for him to follow her to one side out of the way. She pulled her phone out. "I'm supposed to call the receptionist."

"Are we meeting a receptionist? I bet they get all the best court gossip," Osian whispered when Abra hushed him. "What?"

Abra finished up the call then grinned at Osian. "You sound like you're talking about we're off to see the queen or something. Court gossip."

"What else would you call it when someone's sharing rumours here?"

They argued over court gossip for several minutes until a young person came to guide them beyond the public area through the labyrinth of corridors. They reached the door to one of the many judges' chambers of suites. *High Court Judge Leetha Abbey. Who are we questioning?*

Osian read the name on the door a few times before stepped into the reception area. He nudged Abra with his elbow. "You failed to mention we were going to ask a high court judge probing questions."

"I'd prefer not to be probed."

"I apologise, your ladyship." Abra subtly stamped on Osian's foot when he snickered. "Auntie Sue never mentioned who exactly we'd be meeting."

"I'm only 'her ladyship' in court. Please call me Leetha." Judge Abbey waved away the apology. "Why don't you both join me in my office? Less chance of us being overheard."

The office seemed straight out of a Pinterest barrister aesthetic board. One wall was covered entirely by shelves filled to the brim with old law books. The judge settled into her plush leather chair behind her solid antique desk.

Osian glanced at the expensive carpet underneath his shoes and realised he'd definitely underdressed for the occasion. After Abra introduced both of them, he filled the judge in very briefly on what they were doing. "Abs's auntie thought you might offer insights into Hamnet Allsop."

"We called him Hands Hamnet at university." She twisted around in her chair, reaching down to retrieve a leather photo album from one of the lower shelves. "He was two years ahead of me at Cambridge. Thankfully, he never seemed interested in me. I didn't have the right family name, connections, or money. Even now, that hasn't changed much."

"Did Judge Allsop have any issues with Barnaby Sharrow?" Abra asked.

"I suppose it would depend on your definition of

issue." Leetha offered a wry smile. She flipped through the pages in the album, stopping on one about halfway through. "We were all appointed to the judiciary around the same time. Sue and I were the only women of colour. And two of three women in a much larger group of men."

Osian leaned in closer to inspect the photo. "Do you believe Hamster was having an affair?"

"Oz." Abra shook her head, then glanced over at the judge, who'd begun to chuckle. She rolled her eyes at Osian. "Why do you never have a sense of decorum?"

"Olivia got all of it." Osian sat back in his chair, not wanting to crowd the desk. "I'm sure you hate to speak ill of the dead or of another judge. But would you anyway?"

Leetha pulled her album back across the desk; her eyes glinted with amusement. "Barnaby Sharrow and I never had much interaction outside of the usual. I'm not as fond of parties and mingling as some of my fellow judges. He seemed a competent barrister for the most part, perhaps distracted in the last few weeks of his life."

The judge clicked through the pages of the photo album. She seemed to be considering something. Her fingers rested against a particular image for a few seconds.

"You'll step on a number of well-connected toes if you poke your nose around these hallowed halls too much." Leetha eventually closed the album. "I have no idea who murdered poor Barnaby Sharrow. Your friend Wayne seems an improbable candidate even with the overwhelming evidence."

"A few mashed toes never killed anyone," Osian joked, though he did take her warning to heart. "Who do you think we should poke first?"

"You're looking for someone who had the most to lose with Barnaby alive and Wayne free. Enough for them to risk being caught in the act of murder." Leetha paused when a knock sounded. One of her clerks popped in to remind of her a meeting. She waited until the door shut to continue. "Or, perhaps, a person so accustomed to their position of privilege they'd never even consider being found out or punished. They quite literally believe they can get..."

"Away with murder." Osian knew the type. He'd run into them often enough as a paramedic. "We'll be cautious."

Abra snorted beside him.

"What? I can be cautious."

Abra coughed a few times, the last sounding suspiciously like the words "Down a well."

"Rude."

Leaving the judge to her meeting and Abra to head off to work, Osian walked to the police station in the hopes of speaking with Wayne. He wanted to know more about the judge and his philandering ways. The journey gave him time to consider the best approach to convincing one of the detective inspectors into letting him in to see their suspect.

"No."

"I haven't even said anything." Osian had barely made it halfway up the steps to the police station when Haider came down the steps toward him. "Busy day?"

Haider sighed so deeply that he sounded like a pierced balloon. He finally motioned for Osian to follow him. "Let's grab a coffee. Maybe it'll get me through the rest of the day."

"How've you been? How's the wife and kids? Hasn't the weather been lovely?"

"First, I'm desperately in need of a holiday. Second, I've no wife or kids, as you well know." Haider jogged across the street with Osian following close behind. "It's been raining all day. Why don't you get to the point?"

"I'm hurt." Osian feigned outrage. "I thought we were friends."

The grumbling detective shouldered his way through a throng of people and led the way into the café. They waited ten minutes before they managed to get coffees and pastries. Osian opted for a sausage roll.

He considered continuing with small talk, but Haider was likely to be most receptive while enjoying his break. "Any word on my favourite solicitor?"

"Wayne Dankworth should be out soon. He's not been charged." Haider glared at him over the rim of his coffee cup. "And no, I can't tell you anything else about the case or why we've released him."

"I sense you mean 'hasn't been charged *yet*,' am I right?" Osian noticed the tightening around Haider's mouth.

"We'll be thorough in our investigation as always. No arrests have been made. Nor will they be until we're certain," Haider promised. He paused for another sip of coffee. "Try not to get yourself into trouble. Maybe leave the police work to the professionals."

"Me and my sausage roll practice safe..." Osian

trailed off, snickering. "I won't fall into any wells or get myself electrocuted by a ghost."

Haider smiled briefly before turning serious. "How have your dreams been?"

Osian's smile became a little forced. "I haven't turned into Mystic Meg."

"Osian."

"The nightmares have stopped mostly." He shrugged. "Therapy does help. The group you introduced me to helped as well. Pity there's not an instant cure for post-traumatic stress. I'm doing better, though. Promise."

"Small steps." Haider patted him on the shoulder. "I should get back to my desk. I imagine you'll see your solicitor friend in less than an hour. Try to resist the urge to poke your nose into this one. Please."

"Sure," Osian lied through his teeth with a convincing smile.

TEN

DANNEL

"Rolly?" Dannel had watched his brother for several minutes in concern. They'd gotten out of the car, and Roland had frozen, staring up at the building. "Are you all right?"

"All my life, I've wanted to be a police officer. I dedicated myself to helping my community. Closest I could ever come to being a superhero." Roland shoved his hands into his pockets, breathing out through his mouth harshly. "I believe in justice and due process. What if an innocent man gets convicted of murder?"

"It wouldn't be the first time. Not everyone's as dedicated to the truth as you are." Dannel immediately wanted to kick himself when his brother's shoulders drooped. Roland needed positivity and hope, not brutal practicality. "Haider's a decent bloke. Clever. He's not likely to close his case without digging deeper to find the truth."

"Or he might decide they already have the answers," Roland retorted morosely. He shook his head after a moment. "Come on, then. Let's see if anyone saw anything useful."

Given the time of day, Dannel wondered how many people would be home. His heart began to race a little at the prospect of knocking on doors and questioning complete strangers. It wasn't one of his talents.

Even as a firefighter, Dannel had struggled with dealing with the public. In the heat of the moment, he could focus on saving lives and stopping fires. After, he'd never done brilliantly chatting with victims of whatever incident.

Sometimes I don't even want to talk to Ossie, and I love him with my entire being.

Some days are nonverbal ones.

"Where do we start?" Dannel had begun to wonder if they could actually go door to door without someone reporting them as a nuisance. "Can you get in trouble for interfering in an investigation that's not officially assigned to you?"

"Probably." Roland started to walk toward the

building. "I've an idea to keep us out of trouble with Haider."

"Oh?" Dannel wasn't worried about himself, but Roland had a career to consider. "What's the plan?"

"Mrs Rose."

"Who's Mrs Rose?"

"Lives on the first floor. Woman who knows more about what happens around here than CCTV does." Roland paused in the middle of the parking area, glancing around at the vehicles. "We'll likely find her in the garden. She has a small section all her own."

From his brother's brief description, Dannel had an image of what Mrs Rose would be like. She turned out to be a spry seventy-something-year-old with bright green hair, wearing a T-shirt with the colours of the lesbian flag, and carrying a watering can in her hand. She waved cheerfully at Roland.

"Hello, handsome. Have they let your solicitor out on good behaviour yet?" She set the watering can down on the ground. "They haven't, have they? Typical. Why don't we chat over some of my special tea?"

Leading the way up to her first-floor flat, Mrs Rose left them in her cosy sitting room while she got the kettle going. Dannel inspected the various photos covering one of the walls. All of Mrs Rose at various ages with other women at clubs, rallies, and protests.

"I'm what they used to call a spinster, because I refused to marry the man my parents approved of." Mrs Rose motioned for Roland to take the tray with the cups and saucers into the room. "We've progressed so far as a society with so much more to accomplish. My Josie and I were married the moment it became possible."

Special tea appeared to be heavily laced with some sort of whisky. Dannel's eyes watered when he took a sip. He gently set the cup down on the saucer.

"Dannel's going to marry his childhood sweetheart soon." Roland patted him on the shoulder, then went to sit down across from Mrs Rose, who'd chosen what was obviously her favourite chair.

"Wayne's such a good lad. He's always checked in on Josie and me." Mrs Rose settled into her seat. "Now. How can I help you?"

Roland paced by the window, staring out into the garden. "Did you see anything the other night?"

"Hmm." Mrs Rose directed Roland to a notebook visible on a desk across the room. "Everyone needs a hobby. Mine is gardening and being nosy."

"I've seen worse hobbies." Roland brought the book over to her.

Taking the notebook from him, Mrs Rose turned a few pages and found one for the day of the murder. Dannel tried to read the flowery script upside down. He couldn't make out much more than the times running along the right side of the paper.

"Ah, here we go. You and Wayne arrived quite sloshed. We heard you singing in the lift. A rousing rendition of 'You'll Never Walk Alone.'" Mrs Rose covered her mouth when she laughed. "WA from the sixth floor drove you. I saw her leave with Wayne's vehicle for a while. She came back with a rather tall bloke an hour later. I dozed off, so I've no idea if they left again."

"Did you recognise the bloke?" Dannel asked. He hadn't dared touch his tea again, since liquid courage would make his mind fuzzy. "Does he live in the building?"

"I've never seen him before. He reminded me of one of those buff military types." She held the page of her book out so Roland could take a photo with his phone. "I tried telling the young constable who questioned me that morning. They didn't seem inclined to believe me."

"Typical." Dannel wasn't surprised. He imagined the constable had written Mrs Rose off after one look at her wild hair and unusual journal. "We are inclined to believe you."

"Excellent. Now, why don't you two pop off to solve crimes?" She ushered them out of her flat. "My garden won't water itself."

They said goodbye and made their way up to Wayne's flat. The police tape had been removed. Dannel assumed the detectives had finished combing through every inch of the place.

Roland led him inside, stopping in the middle of the living room. "They were certainly thorough."

"Were you robbed?" Dannel wondered if a cyclone had blown through. Papers were scattered everywhere. "Can a room be dishevelled?"

Roland sank down on the sofa, ignoring the papers underneath him. He massaged his temples with a groan. "You don't have to clean."

Unable to think clearly in the clutter, Dannel began to gather up all the loose papers. He organised them into stacks on the coffee table. It wasn't perfect but certainly better than before.

Dannel sat across from Roland, bending down to pick up a stray receipt. "So, Willa?"

"Willa." Roland dropped his hands away from his face. "I doubt she'll be as open or friendly as Mrs Rose."

"Think Ossie got in to see Wayne?" Dannel had been waiting to get a text from Osian. He stared at his phone, willing it to buzz. "How do we question Willa?"

"We don't. She'll see me coming a mile away."

"Yet another phrase that makes no sense. You have to get up close to chat with someone, so what does it matter if they see you coming?" Dannel considered if one of their friends might have better luck. "Maybe Abra and Ossie can chat with her? Willa didn't seem to mind speaking with him the other morning."

"True." Roland stretched his legs out on the coffee table. He dislodged one of the stacks, grinning when Dannel grumbled at him. "Wayne hadn't been taken in for questioning on a murder then. Willa might not be so chatty now."

"We—" Dannel cut himself off when his phone beeped. He checked the message, immediately relieved to see one from Osian. The long delay had begun to worry him. "Ossie managed to speak with Haider. Wayne's being released."

"Let's go." Roland was up off the sofa before Dannel had a chance to respond to Osian's text. "Come on."

Dannel followed his brother down to the parking lot. "Are you okay to drive?"

"I'll be fine."

The short drive to the police station went by in total silence. Roland constantly tapping his fingers against the steering wheel was the only sound. Dannel kept an eye on his brother in concern.

He'd never seen Roland so anxious.

Quiet comfort was all Dannel had to offer. The ride felt like they'd gone all the way to Scotland. They finally arrived, finding Osian and Wayne chatting on the pavement outside the station.

"Wayne," Roland whispered. He quickly found a place to park, then practically ran at light speed to his boyfriend, throwing his arms around him. "Thank everything."

"Thank Bradley's brilliant barrister mind." Wayne nodded to Dannel when he waved. "I hear you've all been quite busy."

"We couldn't let you languish in jail." Dannel tried to keep the mood light and not bring attention to his brother's obvious relief. He hoped it was that and not distress. "Wait until we tell you what we found out today. Also, you might want to have someone in to help you clean up your flat. They left quite a mess for you."

"Why don't we all talk over a late lunch? I'm starved. Microwave meals just aren't the same." Wayne kept an arm around Roland when he finally released him from his tight hug. "Somewhere far away from the police station."

"There's a funeral at Westminster Cathedral tomorrow. Open to the public." Osian sipped from his cup of coffee, following them to where Roland had parked the car. "Think anyone would mind if we went?"

"Just try not to get yourself arrested." Wayne sounded tired. "It wouldn't be the first time."

"Small detail."

ELEVEN

OSIAN

"No Dannel?" Chris met Osian outside Westminster Cathedral. They'd arrived early for the funeral. "Dankworth decided showing up might cause a scene, considering everything. So it's just you and me."

"Dannel decided he didn't have the energy to deal with strangers today. Ready for a bit of sleuthing?" Osian fidgeted with his tie. "Rubbing noses with the toffs who'd probably have sneered at us at university?"

"First, you didn't go to university with any of these people." Chris paused to allow a well-dressed couple to pass by them. He dropped his voice lower, leaning into Osian. "Second, what makes you think I wasn't one of the toffs?"

"Sodding James Bond," Osian grumbled. "One day, you'll give us the whole back story and not drips and drabs of it."

He smirked in response.

Chris Kirwin had been in the military. Osian had the distinct feeling he'd been some sort of special operative. They'd probably never know the whole story.

Then again, it wasn't theirs to know.

Rolling his eyes at his friend, Osian figured he could still poke at him. Their personal man of mystery. *Maybe I do play too many video games.*

"A lot of important people in here," Osian muttered. They grabbed spots on the benches closest to the exit. "Judges, see a couple of MPs, high-ranking members of all the emergency services, might even be a minor royal. How connected are the Sharrows?"

"More than I am."

"You sure? You could be the illegitimate child of some old duke," Osian teased.

"Not that I'm aware of. My—"

Osian gently nudged Chris's arm to shut him up. "Am I hallucinating?"

Chris followed his gaze across the nave toward

the couple strolling down the aisle. "No, no, you're not. Judge Allsop does indeed appear to be playing escort to the grieving widow."

"To her husband's funeral? Isn't he married? Where's his wife?" Osian peered around the cathedral. He noticed several other heads had turned, watching the progression. "Gossip will be flying around the Crown Court water cooler tomorrow."

"There's the wife." Chris nodded his head. "On the arm of one of their private security team."

"Seriously?" Osian couldn't keep his eyes off the public spectacle. "Can you imagine how uncomfortable the ride in their Rolls-Royce was?"

"People like them spend their entire lives ignoring uncomfortable conversations and awkward moments." Chris sounded so painfully familiar that Osian decided not to ask questions.

The funeral was as dull as Osian anticipated, aside from the initial drama. They didn't learn anything useful from the speeches aside from people being terrible liars about their grief. Crying without tears, singing Barnaby's praises without mentioning a single actual memory or moment. And it was long.

Long and boring.

He had flashbacks to lectures at school without

the side of sleuthing. As the service wrapped up, a quiet scuffle caught their attention. Security appeared to be strong-arming a man out of the church.

Osian hadn't been able to catch a glimpse of his face. Security did a masterful job of getting the intruder outside before anyone other than those at the back noticed. They were obviously professionals.

The three men had come with Judge Allsop. He seemed intent on everyone being aware of his general importance. A flashy car, private security, striding through a funeral with the dead man's wife.

"Chris." Osian itched to get up and catch a look at the man's face.

"We can't sneak out now. It'll be way too obvious." Chris put a hand out to stop him from getting up. "I recognised one of the security detail. I'll text him. He might tell us what happened."

"Might?"

"Depends on how he feels about Allsop." Chris shrugged.

"How would you feel? Working for the handsy hamster?" Osian had no doubts those who worked in security gossiped amongst each other like paramedics did after rough days on the job. "Would your friend share with you? After a security detail?"

"We talk with each other when we can't go to anyone else." Chris continued typing out a message on his phone. "We'll see if the fish takes the bait. Maybe we can meet at one of the nearby pubs."

Thankfully for his burning curiosity, the speeches finally wrapped up. Osian didn't know if he could sit through much more. They waited for the church to empty.

The slow procession of guests took forever. Everyone wanted a moment with the widow and the grieving family. Both equally. Making nice to make an impression. Osian had seen it before.

"He's taking a quick break and will meet us in twenty." Chris pocketed his phone and nudged Osian with his elbow. "He wasn't supposed to be working today, apparently. So job's done when the client's gone."

"Enough time to eavesdrop on a few conversations. Pay our respects." Osian got to his feet with a groan. He stretched a little, trying to relax his muscles. "Is this why they call it penance? Sitting on benches meant to numb your bum?"

Stepping out of the church, they saw no signs of the funeral crasher or the security who'd hustled him out of sight. *How very efficient of them.* Osian followed Chris through the motions of blending in with the crowd of mourners, making all the appropriate remarks to the grieving family.

They didn't learn anything earth-shattering.

Osian joined Chris on the pavement down from the church, out of hearing of the crowd of mourners. "Okay, James Bond of the toffs. What do we do next?"

"Why don't we head to the pub?" Chris tugged at his tie, loosening it a little. "I'm parched."

They were almost at the pub when a sharp whistle drew them to the alley beside it. Chris went over for what Olivia would've called a chummy man-hug. They patted each other on the back and separated.

Ah, yes, we've stumbled upon the dark underworld of private security in the wild. Let's observe their secret mating rituals.

Chris narrowed his eyes when Osian couldn't hold back a chuckle. "I'm sure I don't want to know what you're thinking. Robert, meet Osian. Osian, Robert."

"Pleasure."

Osian shook the hand held out to him. "Any particular reason we aren't currently sitting in comfortable chairs waiting for our beers to arrive?"

"Questions about Crown Court judges don't get asked in pubs." Robert kept his voice low and his eyes on the end of the alley. "I'm not getting myself sacked while trying to repay a favour."

"Don't be dramatic." Chris leaned against the wall.

Robert scowled at Chris for a few seconds. "I've no idea who killed Barnaby Sharrow. I've said as much to the police. And I've no clue who the bloke crashing the funeral was. He claimed to be a client. Ed handled him."

"Ed?" Osian asked.

"Edgar Smith. He's in charge of Judge Allsop's security detail." Robert peered around Chris down the alley and lowered his voice further. "He also happens to be the son of the judge's closest childhood friend. Sir something or another. They're all ridiculously wealthy and connected. The kind of people who don't think the rules apply to them."

"But want to enforce the same rules onto others. I know the type. And I know Ed." Chris completed the thought. "Anything you can tell us about the man at the funeral?"

"No. Ed seemed to be expecting him." Robert shrugged. "Ask him at your own risk."

"You worried about Eddie Smith? Really?"

Osian watched the two men bicker back and forth about Edgar Smith and whether they should be concerned about him for several minutes. "We're trying to help a friend."

"I don't know what to tell you. Judge Allsop isn't my usual detail. I'm usually not even in London, so I can't offer you anything concrete." Robert checked his watch. "And I'm late."

"Rob?" Chris grabbed his arm when he went by. "Let me know?"

"Sure."

After Robert had disappeared, Chris motioned for Osian to follow him. They walked to a car park not far from the cathedral. It didn't take long to reach Chris's vehicle.

"So, what was the big favour he owed you?" Osian asked once they'd gotten into Chris's Range Rover. "Big enough he'd risk his job?"

"I took a bullet for him." Chris started the vehicle without another word. "And I've no interest in talking about it."

"Sodding James Bond," Osian grumbled. "What about this Edgar Smith? Could he tell us about how Barnaby died? Maybe about the mystery man at the funeral?"

"Why don't we see if Wayne knows any of Barnaby's clients? We might be able to identify him ourselves." Chris hesitated when he went to start his vehicle.

"Problem?"

"Look." Chris gestured across the way. "Someone isn't happy with the judge."

No widow in sight this time. Judge Allsop and his wife appeared to be having the calmest argument Osian had ever seen. No waving hands, no raised voices. If he couldn't see the clearly angry faces, he'd have thought it was just a regular conversation.

One of their security detail rushed them into their Rolls-Royce. The vehicle drove off not long after. Osian would've given anything to be a fly on the wall for the conversation on their way home.

"I'm still parched." Chris finally started his vehicle. "Why don't we swing by somewhere to pick up a takeaway for you and Dannel?"

"What about Edgar Smith?"

"You reach out to Wayne about potential clients. I'll see if I can find a way to leverage Ed into speaking with me." Chris slowly backed out of the parking space. "Patience, Oz. You can't run headlong at a crown court judge or his security detail."

"What can you tell me about him, though?"

"Nothing." Chris waved his hand sharply.

Forty-five minutes later, Osian trudged up the stairs to their flat. He had a bag of food from Nando's. It had been on the way, and Dannel never tired of their chips.

Osian stepped into their flat, only to have Dannel snatch the food out of his hand and immediately search inside the bag. He came out holding a packet triumphantly. "You only love me for my chips."

"Yep. All you're good for is a bit of fried potato on the side." Dannel shoved several in his mouth. "I'm half-starved."

"Forget to eat again?"

"Got distracted working on the designs for this new armour set." Dannel gestured to the sketchbook on the coffee table. "Remember the Nightingale set from *Skyrim*? Something along those lines. We can start fabrication later while you tell me about the funeral."

"After chips?"

"After chips." Dannel hadn't relinquished the packet. "Did you learn anything?"

"I'm fairly certain Chris actually is James Bond." Osian fished into the bag for the second packet of chips. "Or maybe Sam Fisher."

"He's American. And a video game character. And part of a fictional government organisation." Dannel pointed a chip at him. "Chris is real."

"Real dangerous."

TWELVE
DANNEL

DANNEL WOKE UP THE FOLLOWING DAY WITH AN Osian-shaped blanket draped over him. They'd fallen asleep on the couch watching a replay of a football match. His phone buzzed from the coffee table just out of his reach. "Ossie?"

Osian snored in response.

"Ossie?" Dannel shook him gently.

"Wha—" Osian shot up out of his deep sleep, forcing Dannel to catch him before he hit the floor. "Are we late?"

"Can you grab my phone?"

"Seriously?" Osian grumbled. He yawned, stretched, and finally reached out to grab Dannel's phone. "Here."

"Roland sent a text." Dannel quickly scrolled

through the multiple messages from his brother. "The helpful neighbour we met? She sent him a photo of the guy with Willa. Wayne recognised him from Crown Court."

Osian leaned across Dannel to get a view. "He was at the funeral; part of the security team."

"Edgar Smith." Dannel pushed away the uneasy feeling building in his chest and read the rest of the message from his brother. "He's in charge of Judge Allsop's security."

"Wait. Willa Abraham and Edgar Smith had control of Wayne's vehicle the night a dead body was shoved into it?" Osian slipped off Dannel and sat up on the couch. He leaned sleepily against him. "Is Roland sending the photo to Haider? I can't imagine the detective inspectors won't be interested in new evidence."

"What's the phrase we heard on telly the other day? Fruit of the poisonous tree? Will they believe anything coming from Rolly?" Dannel wasn't sure they would. "Maybe Mrs Rose can reach out herself. It might be better coming from her directly. He wants to know if we're up for meeting him and Wayne for breakfast."

"I suppose the question is, were they both involved?" Osian pushed himself up off the couch, reaching back to hold a hand out to Dannel. "We should shower if we're going out for breakfast. Want to help me wash my back?"

"We have one of those long things that helps... Not what you meant." Dannel allowed himself to be dragged through the flat to indulge their favourite early morning wake up—an extra-long shower.

I'm fine. There's nothing to stress over. We're only having coffee with Rolly and Wayne.

They were thirty minutes late for their breakfast. Wayne and Roland had picked a quiet coffee shop around the corner from the court. Dannel ignored their knowing looks.

"Edgar Smith." Dannel got straight to the point once they'd gotten their orders in for coffee and breakfast. "What do you know about him?"

"He's connected," Wayne responded after a few seconds of hesitation.

"If I hear that word one more time...." Osian dragged a hand across his face. "The judge. The barrister. The dead barrister. The judge's security. The first thing anyone thinks to say about any of them is they're connected."

"Thought you didn't want to hear the word?" Roland grinned at him. "You know what the people at the top are like, Oz. How many of them did you run into as a paramedic? Patching them up after a drunken incident, yet no police investigated. I've seen it."

"Bradley said Edgar got the job because of Judge Allsop." Osian swapped half his sandwich with Dannel, who winked at him. "We should ask Chris. I got the feeling he's known the man for a while."

"Family friend?" Dannel asked.

"A lot of those going around." Wayne leaned back in his chair.

"Well?"

"Well, what?" Wayne glanced over at Osian.

"Edgar Smith?"

"Tall, bulky bloke who'd look right at home on a rugby pitch." Wayne waved the barista over, asking for a top-up of his coffee. He raised an eyebrow when both Dannel and Osian stared at him. "What?"

Dannel looked closely at their solicitor friend. His shirt was rumpled, tie loosened, and his usually perfect hair mussed up. He seemed exhausted and not himself. "You all right, Wayne?"

"Tired." Wayne tapped his finger against the rim of his coffee cup. "I had to run into the office to grab some files."

"Are you going to court? Has something happened with the murder investigation?" Dannel grew tired of the non-answers. It felt like they were dancing around for no reason. "Why are we here?"

"Danny." Roland snapped at him. "He's having a rough week. We don't all like to dive straight into conversation. A little tact? It's not rocket science."

"Roland." Osian bristled beside Dannel. "Why don't you take a breath? We're trying to help. And subtle small talk is rocket science to some people. Hell, it's practically a whole other language for some."

Roland deflated almost immediately. He sent an apologetic smile to Dannel, who waved it off. "We're having a rough week."

"Barnaby Sharrow had a tougher one." Dannel didn't think his questions had been overly probing. "Pretending things aren't precarious won't help. Until the murder is solved—Wayne's basically a few steps away from a prison sentence."

"Danny." Roland hit his hand on the table. "Seriously?"

"He's not wrong." Osian stepped into the conversation again, placing a hand on Dannel's arm. He focused his question at Wayne. "Did Edgar Smith have a reason to want to get rid of Sharrow? And blame you?"

"No idea." Wayne slowly sat up in the chair. He

ran his fingers through his hair a few times, then straightened his tie. "We've all seen him around. Barnaby had more interactions with the judge and, therefore, with his security detail. I've no doubt they all mingled at private events and dinners—none of which I'd have been invited to. I don't run in those circles."

"Therefore," Osian teased.

"Did Edgar have a reason for a grudge against you?" Dannel asked. He noticed Roland's glare and decided not to take it personally. "I know you're worried about your boyfriend. Quit taking it out on me."

"None of the security at the courthouse has been anything other than professional." Wayne stirred his coffee absently once the barista had topped it off. He added more sugar, staring morosely into the mug. "Edgar was the one to separate Sharrow and Allsop when they had words with each other."

"Had words?" Dannel couldn't help rolling his eyes. "Think there's a point in trying to track Edgar Smith down at the court? Maybe he'll answer a few questions."

"Chris made it seem like he'd need to chat with him first." Osian grabbed his phone from underneath the paper on the table. "Why don't I text him?"

"Court's open to the public." Dannel figured there was no harm in swinging by the hallowed halls of the Old Bailey like a quartet of tourists. "Better than sitting in a coffee shop getting narky with each other."

"I've been informed my presence near the court or my office will only draw unwanted attention." Wayne sipped his coffee, then set the mug down hard enough to slosh liquid over the rim. "Even if they find the killer, my reputation's in tatters. No one's going to remember who actually did it. All they'll see is my being taken in for questioning."

They didn't get a chance to respond. Judie Sharrow swanned into the coffee shop and sucked all the air out of the room. An Hermès scarf and expensive perfume trailed in her wake.

And she wasn't alone.

Edgar Smith followed close behind her. Dannel glanced back at Osian. He had a feeling they all had questions about the two of them.

Why is the security detail for a Crown Court judge following a diary clerk, who happened to be married to a murdered barrister, like an oversized guard dog?

"I so wanted to thank you for attending the funeral yesterday." Judie paused by their table, resting a manicured and bejewelled hand on Osian's shoulder. Her smile became markedly predatory when she spotted Wayne. "Lovely to see you all. Don't be a stranger, Dankworth. One might think you're hiding yourself away."

So.

The wife definitely did it.

Seconds later, Judge Hamnet Allsop stepped into the coffee shop. He walked over to join Judie at the counter. *Turns out we didn't need to visit the court after all; the drama's come to us instead.*

Fascinating.

"They're acting like a married couple." Osian leaned over to whisper in Dannel's ear. "Except he's got a wife on the side, and her husband's barely been in the ground twenty-four hours."

"Don't posh people have mausoleums? He might not actually be in the ground."

"Not actually the point." Osian snickered. He cleared his throat after noticing something behind Dannel. "Incoming judicial confrontation in three seconds."

"Dankworth." Hamnet Allsop sounded like every parody of an aristocrat Dannel had ever seen. He cast a cursory glance around the table before returning his attention to Wayne. "I see they've released you."

"They had no reason to hold me." Wayne lifted his mug up, offering a mock salute to the judge with it. "Thank you for the concern. I wouldn't want to intrude on your... coffee break."

Shifting in his seat slightly, Dannel rolled his shoulders, trying to ease the tension in his chest. The room grew smaller. He closed his eyes for a second and took several measured breaths.

Judge Allsop tilted his head to one side, staring down Wayne. "Careful, Dankworth. We wouldn't want to forever ruin a promising career, would we?"

"Yes, it's always a pity when careers are ruined." Wayne casually sipped his coffee. "How's your wife doing?"

The judge stormed off without answering. Dannel noticed the security detail keeping a close eye on them. He wondered if they hadn't riled up trouble for themselves.

"What a massive knobhead," Osian muttered quietly. He grabbed his phone when it beeped, skimming the message. "Chris wants to meet up in an hour."

And I want to go home.

Dannel continued to take slow breaths. He

jumped a little when Osian wrapped an arm around his shoulders. "I'm fine."

"You're not, actually." Osian always knew when he'd reached the end of his social rope. "Why don't we head home, yeah? I can meet Chris by myself."

"Home." Dannel had definitely reached his limits.

"I've got my 'Dannel relax kit' in the boot of my car." Roland got to his feet. He drained the remnants of his coffee and crouched down next to his brother's chair. "Listen, I'm sorry about earlier. I'm worried about Wayne. How about I give you a lift? And our two muppets can meet with Chris."

"I resent muppet." Wayne sent a lazy smile at Roland. "Sounds like a good plan, though."

The relax kit had been an idea of Osian's. Several of their friends and family had them. Small bag with all the things Dannel often used to help ease the strain of a meltdown.

"Home," Dannel repeated.

"Home it is." Osian squeezed his shoulder then eased back from Dannel. "Text me if you need anything. Chris can always wait if you want me, okay?"

"Fine." Dannel shrugged.

Putting words together was hard. Dannel trusted

Osian to deal with things. He wanted time to himself. Alone with music and a heavy blanket until the weight moved off his chest and his mind went back to processing things going on around him.

"I love you." Osian gave him one last hug, then shoved him gently toward Roland. "I'll bring chips and cake."

"The cure to all problems." Roland chuckled.

THIRTEEN
OSIAN

"I'll grab us two more coffees to go." Wayne returned to the coffee shop, leaving Osian outside watching the Ortea brothers walk down the pavement.

Taking a seat on a nearby bench, Osian decided to check in with Abra. He figured her godmum might have more insights to share. A slim chance, given her earlier reluctance.

"Here." Wayne sat next to him, stretching his legs out in front. "Will Dannel be okay?"

"What? Sure. He'll be fine." Osian trusted Dannel to decompress from the day in his own way. He often found their friends and family struggled to simply allow him the time. "What about you? Will you be okay?"

He didn't get a chance to answer when his phone rang. Osian tried not to seem obvious while listening to the call. It was impossible to offer privacy when Wayne was sitting right beside him.

"I'll be there as soon as I can." Wayne ended the call, then gripped his phone tightly in his hand. "The police apparently have more questions for me. Bradley's meeting me there."

"Bugger. Want me to go with you?"

"No. Meet with Chris. Maybe the police will move on if they have an actual suspect?" Wayne stood up and strode away from him.

Haider and I are going to have a really long conversation. How the hell can he still think Wayne's a suspect?

If Osian were being generous, he would admit to understanding the police suspicions. No matter his firm beliefs on Wayne's innocence, the evidence didn't really help matters. *We're going to solve this.*

"Where's Dankworth?" Chris jogged toward him, dropping onto the bench with a grunt. "You're lucky I've a day off."

"Since when do you take a day off?"

"Family stuff." Chris shrugged.

"So, what's the deal with Edgar Smith?" Osian refused to waste time beating around the bush.

124

"Why are you so squirrely when his name comes up? Unrequited love?"

"Please stop talking. I do not need those visuals in my head." Chris shuddered dramatically before glancing at his phone. "Edgar and I have history. I asked him to meet us."

"Yes, I figured that out all on my own, given your reaction to him."

Chris sighed, shifting on the bench and folding his arms across his chest. "Our families are—"

"I swear if you say connected, I will take my chances and take a swing at you," Osian grumbled.

"Edgar and I have a half-sister in common. My father. His mother, technically my stepmother."

Osian held up a hand to stop Chris. He mentally repeated what his friend had said five times and still didn't think he'd fully understand. "I'm sorry. What?"

"My father and his current wife grew up together along with Edgar's father. They had one of those rom-com-like love triangles, you know? It got complicated." Chris ran his fingers through his hair, making a mess of it. "There was an ugly divorce. Then another marriage."

"Is there something in the water at your schools?"

"Maybe." Chris snorted with laughter. "Listen, Edgar's father and mine went to school with Judge Allsop. Birds of a feather flock together."

"They certainly do something together." Osian decided not to delve too deeply into the subject. "Wait. You have a sister?"

"Tamsyn. Nine years younger than me. She lives in Florida." Chris grabbed his phone, scrolling through his photos before showing Osian an image of a young woman on a fishing boat. "They sent her away to live with a family friend. Part of the divorce settlement when Tamsyn refused to pick between her mother or father."

"Are you close?"

Chris nodded his head, grinning at Osian. "We are. She's the only person in my family that I'd actually claim. Dannel reminds me of her sometimes."

"Oh?"

"She's autistic." Chris pocketed his phone. "Edgar and I had a falling out about ten years ago. He wanted her to move to London and claimed we should keep a closer eye on her. I believed she was happy and a grown adult capable of making her own decisions. She still is."

"And the falling out involved?"

"Edgar tried to bully her into moving here."

126

Chris was silent for several minutes before continuing. "I went above and beyond to ensure he left her alone."

"You 'had words'?"

"More than."

Osian decided not to shove his nose further into Chris's personal business for the moment. He redirected the conversation slightly. "Is Edgar capable of murdering someone and setting Wayne up?"

"Capable? Definitely." Chris checked his phone once again. "What's his motivation, though?"

"Good question."

They sat for another twenty minutes before Chris received another text. He motioned for Osian to follow him. They made their way a few blocks down from the Old Bailey.

"A secret meeting in a secluded section of a parking garage?" Osian couldn't help grinning at Chris. "Very James Bond of you."

"One of these days, you're going to get tired of the jokes and let go of this bizarre notion about my life." Chris yanked open the door leading to the staircase. "I'm betting he's already waiting for us."

They jogged up the four flights of stairs. Edgar Smith, dressed in a perfectly fitted suit, stood waiting for them by his Range Rover. Osian definitely felt like an extra in a spy film.

As an unbiased observer, Osian thought Chris and Edgar greeted each other cautiously, like two people playing hot potato with a live grenade. He wondered if one wrong move would lead to an explosion. *I'm not sure I want to be in the range of the blast if they go at it.*

"Kirwin."

"Smith." Chris bit out the word through clenched teeth.

"Garey," Osian added cheerfully. They both glared at him. "What? Is this some bizarre boarding school greeting ritual a lowly little pleb like myself wouldn't understand?"

"We keep the secret handshake to ourselves." Chris shoved his hands in his pockets, returning his attention to Edgar. "How've you been?"

"You don't care."

"I don't, actually."

Osian watched the stoically bizarre verbal tennis match for a few minutes. He was getting bored with the posturing. "If this were a musical, you'd have broken into song by now."

"How about getting to the point?" Edgar had the stance and bearing of someone used to utilising their size to intimidate. He loomed over Osian, who merely smiled lazily up at him. "Well?"

Edgar and Chris were about the same size. Tall, broad-shouldered men. They held themselves the way most soldiers did. Strong, capable, dangerous.

The difference between the two was Chris had never used either his size or training to intimidate others. On the other hand, Edgar struck Osian as someone who would relish the opportunity to do so. A bully. He didn't know if the man had killed Barnaby Sharrow, but he had no doubts Edgar was capable of it.

But what was his motivation? Helping his boss? Was it enough to commit murder?

"Seen Willa Abraham recently?" Osian had a feeling a direct question might end the conversation before they even started.

"Who?" Edgar lied so easily and confidently that Osian was tempted to believe him despite having seen photos to the contrary. "No idea who you're talking about."

"The woman you came home with the night of Sharrow's murder." Chris leaned against the side of the Range Rover.

"Ah. Her." Edgar sniffed dismissively. "Never knew her name."

"And yet you were in Wayne's car with her?"

"And?" Edgar shrugged. "Thought it was hers. Do you ask your dates who owns their vehicle? Odd kink to have, isn't it?"

"Did you?" Osian didn't buy his story.

"I did." Edgar moved his cold, unbothered gaze from Osian to Chris. "How's Tamsyn? Enjoying life in Florida? Maybe I should visit. It's been a long time since I saw our little sister."

Osian watched his friend's eyes go dark. He started forward toward Edgar, who laughed in his face. "Chris."

"You have a good day." Edgar didn't seem worried about Chris in the slightest.

Before they could respond, Edgar got into his Range Rover and swiftly drove away. Osian placed a hand on Chris's shoulder. The conversation had definitely not gone to plan.

"Oz?"

"Yeah?"

"You're my alibi if he goes missing." Chris strode toward the stairs, forcing Osian to jog to catch up to him. "I've genuinely no idea if he murdered Sharrow and framed Dankworth."

"But?"

"We're going to find out for certain one way or

the other." Chris yanked the door open, and it clanged against the cement wall. "I'll make a few calls and see if any of my mates have heard anything. If Dannel's up for it, I can bring over pizza and beer while we try to sift through what information we have."

"He's Kirwin. Chris Kirwin." Osian snickered at the glare sent his way.

And if looks could kill, I'd be worried.

FOURTEEN

DANNEL

AFTER SPENDING AN HOUR UNDER BLANKETS with the *Hamilton* cast album on repeat, Dannel extricated himself from the sofa. Finally, he was ready to shake off his earlier stress completely. *I wonder if Osian and Chris learnt anything from Edgar Smith.*

I should've gone.

No, I shouldn't have. The hardest part of self-care was acknowledging when he needed a break. But, after leaving firefighting behind, he'd gotten better at it.

Better at listening to himself.

Better at setting and respecting his own boundaries.

Heading into the kitchen, Dannel got the electric

kettle going. A fresh mug of coffee would help get him going. It certainly wouldn't hurt.

He had loads of googly eyes to paint to fit as rivets on the armour. The gauntlets, greaves, and chest plate were already formed and hardened. They had one last coat of paint to go as well before the aged patina would be perfect.

Coffee in hand, Dannel retreated to their workroom. He brought their Bluetooth speaker with him, placing it on the desk beside his mug. Nothing cleared the mind like hours spent on the mind-numbing task of painting tiny domes.

By the time he'd finished the coffee, Dannel was ready for a break. His fingers needed a rest. He'd just begun to wash the dishes accumulated in the sink when the doorbell rang.

Dannel dried his hands off on his jeans and went to answer the door, frowning when he found his father on the other side. "Myron?"

"Son. Can I come in?"

No.

"Sure." Dannel stepped back to allow him inside. "I meant to call after you left. Things have been busy."

Only partially a lie. Dannel had meant to reach out after his father's last visit. It likely wouldn't have been a phone call, though. Talking over the phone was slow torture best avoided at all costs. Dannel would've texted his dad eventually. They needed to talk.

But murder was so distracting.

"Are you doing better today?" Myron followed him into the kitchen, taking a seat at the table. "How goes the wedding planning?"

"Better is debatable." Dannel grabbed the kettle to refill it for a second time. "Planning is also debatable. We've decided to let Olivia handle the details."

"Smart lads. She always had a good head on her shoulders, even as a toddler." He chuckled. "However and whenever the wedding happens, I want to be there for you as your dad... if you'll let me."

"Who else would you be there as?" Dannel grabbed a couple clean mugs along with their box of teabags. "I didn't think you'd want to come, since I'm marrying Osian."

"I'm aware of who you're marrying." Myron held a hand up when Dannel went to respond. "I'll never think anyone's good enough for my son. Maybe he'll grow on me."

"Who's better than Ossie?" Dannel couldn't conceive of anyone ever being better than Osian. "He's my best friend."

"You shared crayons."

"What?" Dannel hunted around for their container of sugar cubes. He eventually found it hidden behind a box of cereal in the wrong cabinet. *Damn it, Ossie.* "Crayons?"

"As a kid, you hated sharing them. Neither I, your mum, or even your brother could touch them." Myron leaned back in the chair. He scratched absently at the side of his jaw, watching Dannel fuss around with the tea. "Osian always got your best crayons."

"Osian gets the best of me because he sees the best in me." Dannel poured the boiling water into the mugs. "In us."

"I thought he'd break your heart," Myron admitted after several moments of silence. "I hoped to save you the trouble."

"Ossie? Break my heart?" Dannel would've laughed if his father didn't seem quite so serious. "He doesn't have it in him."

"I'm aware. Now, at least."

Sipping his tea, Dannel had no idea what to say. He wasn't used to having a conversation with Myron without raised voices and hurt feelings. Maybe they'd both grown up.

His father might be years older, but he'd always

need to grow up more than his son. The hesitation he felt about inviting Myron to the wedding faded away. Dannel hoped this marked a fundamental change in their relationship going forward.

"Why don't I head out?" Myron drained the rest of his tea. He got to his feet, pausing to pat Dannel once on the shoulder then heading for the door. "Thanks for the brew."

"Myron." Dannel shifted uneasily. "Dad?"

"Son?"

"Why don't you have dinner with us?" Dannel didn't know if it was a good idea, but Osian had encouraged him to try with his dad. "Next week?"

"I'd love to."

With the flat to himself, Dannel fell back on the sofa with an exhausted groan. His mum would be thrilled with their progress. He'd managed to find common ground with his father.

No one ever tells you being an adult is going to be such an emotional roller coaster.

An hour later, Osian returned with a sack of double chocolate cookies from a nearby American-style bakery. They sat in silence, eating and listening to one of their random playlists. Dannel appreciated not having to immediately jump into a conversation.

He'd already done plenty of talking.

And he kept going back to his chat with his father.

Osian gets the best of me because he sees the best in me.

"Chris has a sister." Osian interrupted his thoughts.

"Really?"

"Edgar threatened her when we met with him." Osian offered Dannel half of the last cookie. "Changed my mind about Chris."

"How so?"

"Less James Bond, more John Wick when threatened." He balled up the now-empty paper bag in his hand. "You up for pizza, beer, and company in a few hours? Chris's buying."

"When have we ever said no to free beer and pizza?"

"Maybe once. Dreadful mistake." Osian leaned against him. "Your uncle caught me on the way up."

"Let me guess. Wanted you to know my dad was up here?" Dannel appreciated his uncle's concern. He also valued Osian's honesty. Another item on the long list of reasons why he loved him so much. They didn't keep secrets. "I invited him to the wedding... and dinner."

"Good."

"I called him 'Dad.'" Dannel laced his fingers with Osian's, resting their joined hands on his leg. "Growing up is a pain in the arse."

"Whether you're thirty or fifty," Osian readily agreed. "So, pizza and plotting with Chris?"

"Fine."

FIFTEEN
OSIAN

"Pizza's here." Osian yelled for Dannel while grinning at Chris, who stood on the other side of the open door. He had four boxes of pizza and a couple six-packs of beer. "If you drop it, we're not paying for it."

"Hilarious. Take the beer?" Chris stepped into the flat, adjusting the boxes when Osian grabbed the two six-packs. "I'm going to need at least one of those."

"Rough day?"

Placing the pizza on the coffee table, Chris grabbed one of the beers. He collapsed on the sofa and slowly drank the entire can. Osian immediately held out a second one to him.

After a few minutes, Dannel joined them. He

was picking bits of paint off his thumb. Osian caught him by the shoulder, directing him into the kitchen to wash his hands.

Retrieving plates from a cabinet, Osian carried them into the living room. They nattered about the previous night's football match over their first bites of pizza. Chris appeared to need time to gather his thoughts.

What better to help than beer, pizza, and footie?

Osian watched Chris begin to pick apart the crust of his pizza. He'd never seen their friend quite so unnerved. "You all right?"

Dannel glanced up from his plate over to Chris. "He looks like he always does. Did I miss something?"

"He looks stressed."

"Does he?" Dannel hunted through the pizza boxes to find another slice of pepperoni. "How can you tell?"

"Who picks apart a pizza crust into tiny pieces?" Osian motioned to Chris's plate. "Plus, he drank his first beer like he'd been in the desert for days."

"Really?"

"Are you two finished analysing me?" Chris interrupted. He seemed more amused than bothered by their banter. "I'm not stressed."

"Uneasy?"

"Uncomfortable?"

"Underrated? No, wait." Osian snickered with Dannel while Chris simply sighed and rested the cold can against his forehead. "What are you if not stressed? Something obviously happened."

Setting his plate to the side, Chris stretched his long legs out. He sighed again. Longer this time, his shoulders slumped, and he dragged his hand across his face.

"Chris?" Osian stopped laughing with Dannel. "What happened? Your sister?"

"She's fine. I texted her earlier." Chris tapped his fingers against the side of his can. "She's annoyed."

"With you?" Osian knew from experience younger siblings could get highly irritated with over-protective brothers. He imagined Chris had the potential to be ten times worse than he was.

"Not with me. I just told her to be careful." Chris sat up straight. "Edgar tried to call her. Twenty times. She counted."

"Twenty? Seems excessive." Dannel took the words out of Osian's mouth.

"Twenty. She never answers calls from anyone. Ever. I have to leave a voice message, and she might call me back. Mostly we text." Chris continued to sip his beer. "She said he never left a message at all. She also reminded me of the mercenary streak running through his veins. Her words."

"Mercenary streak?" Dannel questioned.

"We took slightly different paths after serving in the military. I went into private security immediately. He did anything in the name of money before becoming the personal bodyguard for Allsop." Chris drank the last of his beer and crushed the can in his hand.

"He'd do anything for money?" Osian wondered if that included murder. "Pity we can't see if anyone's dropped a load of cash on him."

"Think Haider would give you an insight into where they're at on the case?" Dannel nudged Osian's leg with his foot.

"I think Haider would give me a long lecture about not getting ourselves into trouble if I try to chat with him about another case." Osian didn't want to push the boundaries of their friendship with the detective inspector too far. "We can, however, try chatting with Willa again."

Chris got to his feet and walked over to look out the window. "She won't talk."

"Why?"

"She's either involved or clever enough to know

she'd be sinking her career down the loo to implicate anyone at the court." Chris twisted around and leaned against the windowsill. "But..."

"But what?" Osian prompted when Chris failed to continue.

"We're still missing out on the key point, in my opinion." Chris twisted around again to stare out the window. "Who had access to Wayne's keys and his tie?"

"Willa seems to have a thing for the tall, strong type. Maybe Chris can ask her a few questions?" Dannel lifted the lids of several of the boxes before selecting another slice of pizza. "She's a solicitor."

"We're aware." Chris's continued focus on the window drew Osian's attention. "Sorry, Dannel. I didn't mean that as narky as it sounded."

"Solicitors aren't prone to answering questions for anyone. Not for real detectives or those playing at it." Dannel made an excellent point. He frowned when Chris simply stared out the window. "What are you staring at?"

"Rolls-Royce parked across the street from your building." Chris knocked his knuckles against the glass. "It keeps popping up."

"Hamster's vehicle?" Osian wandered over to join him.

Staring across the street, Osian spotted the vehicle. It was too dark to say if it really was the same one. *There's no such thing as a coincidence.*

We haven't even stuck our noses too far into the investigation yet.

Abra often told him the more affluent and powerful a person, the bigger their secrets. Barnaby's murder had undoubtedly come with a list of people who fit that criterion. But, unfortunately, one of them seemed to be following them around.

Or having us followed.

"How do we get Willa to chat with us?" Dannel pointed his pizza at Chris. "He might be aesthetically pleasing, but he's not enough of a fox to convince her to share all of her secrets. I doubt anyone is."

"I feel mildly insulted." Chris grinned. "Why don't we try asking her a few questions? The worst she can do is say no. Or tell us to sod off."

"She might do it anyway." Osian had no doubts Willa would stonewall them. "How are we going to convince her to talk with us?"

"Bribe her with Jimmy Choos?" Chris stepped away from the window and headed for the door. "Anyone game to see if the Rolls takes off if we go say a cheery hello to the driver?"

"Why not?" Osian followed him with Dannel close behind. "Who's Jimmy Choo?"

"Shoes."

"He's a shoe?" Dannel sounded as confused as Osian.

"Plebs," Chris teased.

The three made their way down the stairs and out into the crisp night air. Chris strolled casually across the street. Osian was surprised when the Rolls-Royce didn't immediately drive off.

Chris went around to the window, leaning down when it opened. "Edgar. You lost?"

"Just making sure you get home safely." Edgar revved the engine a few times. "London can be such a dangerous place."

"You're a real hero." Chris held a hand up to stop Osian when he moved closer. "Tamsyn wants you to leave her alone."

"Always standing between her and everyone else," Edgar scoffed. He flicked a thumb drive at Chris, who caught it easily. "The judge and his wife weren't anywhere near Dankworth's flat or vehicle. So you should accept the fact that your friend murdered someone. And you should get out of my way before I run you over."

They all stepped back. Edgar revved the engine

a final time before pulling away from the kerb. He disappeared around the corner several seconds later.

"That went well." Osian glanced over at Chris, who shrugged. "So, is he stalking you or us?"

"And what's on the thumb <u>drive</u>?" Dannel added.

"I imagine he's attempting to intimidate all three of us." Chris held up the drive in his hand. "Only one way to find out what's on here."

Retracing their steps, the three men eventually crowded around a laptop. Osian went to slot in the thumb drive when Chris caught his wrist. He grabbed the drive and stared intently at it.

"What?" Osian asked while Chris continued to inspect it.

"Edgar would never voluntarily offer free information without getting something in return. I'm not risking your system's security." Chris slipped the drive into his pocket. "There are any number of viruses he could use. Access to your laptop? Into your life? It wouldn't take much."

"Creepy."

"Welcome to the modern age of stalking and surveillance." Chris winked at him. "Listen, I've got a more secure way to see what Edgar's given us. Why don't we meet up in the morning to track down Willa

Abraham? I'll pop by my office tonight to give this thumb drive to one of our techs."

"Why don't I meet Chris tomorrow?" Dannel tapped Osian on his shoulder. "Aren't you supposed to meet your mum and Olivia to chat about the wedding in the morning?"

"Bugger." Osian rested his head against the table with an exaggerated groan. "Why don't we elope and tell them after?"

"Sure. You get to tell everyone."

"Never mind." Osian liked his body intact. He had no doubts their mums would both be out for blood if they eloped. "Torture by wedding planning it is."

SIXTEEN
DANNEL

Since Osian's mum and sister would show up early to discuss the wedding, Dannel was out the door the following morning with barely a kiss goodbye to his husband-to-be. He didn't want to get roped into the conversation.

"What'd you find?" Dannel greeted Chris with a question when they met outside the tube station near his office. "Anything interesting in the files?"

"Spyware." Chris pulled the drive out of his pocket, this time secured in an evidence bag. "A few blurry images that show nothing at all. Just a ruse to get you to download everything onto your computer."

"Why?" Dannel followed Chris, who began

walking down the street toward where he'd parked his vehicle. "What would the point be?"

Chris stared at Dannel over the top of his sunglasses for several seconds. "Access to whatever you have on your laptop."

"Armour porn?" Dannel grinned. "Seriously? What could he possibly hope to find? We're not the actual police. We've no insight into the investigation."

Chris leaned against the side of his vehicle, tossing his keychain up in the air a few times. "You are investigating."

"Okay. Fair, but if I'd committed murder, I'd want to know what the police had on me." He dug into his pocket for his phone when it beeped. He frowned at the message from his brother. "Rolly's suspension has been upheld—this time without pay."

"What? Why?"

"He has no idea." Dannel quickly typed out a text message to Osian. "Ossie's going to meet with Haider after he's finished with his mum. See if they had something to do with it."

"Haider doesn't seem the type." Chris unlocked his vehicle. "Let's go chase Willa Abraham down. We can meet up with Osian when we're done."

"How are we chasing her down?"

"Let me worry about it." Chris spent the next few minutes on his phone.

Despite Dannel's best efforts, Chris wouldn't explain how he learned where Willa was. Finally, they found her stepping out of her favourite café. Dannel almost regretted seeing her.

He hated confrontation.

"Can I help you?" Willa had her coffee cup in one hand and her phone in the other. "Well? I'm late for a meeting with a client."

"What did you do with Wayne's keys the night of the murder? You had control over them for several hours." Dannel blurted out the question.

"I beg your pardon. How is this any of your business?" She tilted her head to the side, staring at them for several moments before answering. "I left them on my coffee table until Wayne came by looking for them around seven or eight. I can't recall. I was half-asleep when he knocked on my door."

"And Edgar? Was he with you all night?" Chris asked.

Willa narrowed her eyes on them immediately. "That is most certainly not any of your business."

"It's important. Please?" Dannel tried to be disarming. He wasn't sure it worked. "Please?"

Willa sighed. She sipped her coffee. "I don't do

breakfast the next morning with men. He left after we finished. So I went to bed and slept off my evening."

"And the keys were in the same spot you left them?" Chris pressed.

"They were on the coffee table. Unfortunately, I didn't memorise the precise spot." Willa pushed between them to continue down the pavement. "You've made me late. I might bill you."

They watched her saunter off. Dannel had a feeling Edgar had gone to the top of their suspect list. But had he acted alone?

"Do you believe her?" Dannel turned toward the queue for the café. "Want to grab a coffee? I'm thinking about heading over to the police station to speak with Haider. He's closer with Osian, but... I want to know what's going on with Rolly."

"Osian—"

"Ossie is busy distracting our mums and his sister by pretending to agree to their wedding plan ideas." Dannel had a feeling he owed Osian something special for abandoning him to the chaotic madness of their family. "Not sure he'll forgive me by the time the day's over."

"So, basically, he's doing the dirty work."

"Oi. I proposed. That was hard enough." Dannel grinned.

"Hey, check it out." Chris gestured over Dannel's shoulder. "Willa."

They watched her storm down the pavement toward them. Willa had her phone to her ear, shouting at the person at the end of the line. She stalked by them without even acknowledging their presence.

"No, Edgar. I won't calm down."

It was the only part of the conversation they heard. She disappeared around the corner. Dannel glanced over at Chris, who shrugged.

"Trouble in paradise?" Chris muttered. "She's not pleased about something. I'd say we put a fly in the ointment."

"Disgusting."

"But true." Chris checked his watch. "Why don't we grab coffee and doughnuts? Bribe our way into DI Khan's good graces."

"Not sure he has them when it comes to civilians investigating." Dannel wouldn't say no to sugary treats and caffeinated goodness. He grabbed his phone to read the text Osian had sent him. "I am apparently a terrible human being who owes him a full body massage."

"More information than I needed." Chris shook his head.

After grabbing coffee and doughnuts, they made their way to the police station. Dannel felt the awkward silence grow in the vehicle. He almost regretted trading places with Osian.

Almost.

An awkward conversation with a friend was infinitely better than trying to corral the strong women in their lives. *No way. Not happening. I'd wind up agreeing to all their ideas.*

"How's your sister?" Dannel decided to fill the silence with something.

"Grumpy." Chris chuckled. "She changed her phone number so Edgar can't call. Not sure it'll stop him. I might go out to see her."

"Florida?"

"I could use a suntan," Chris revealed, grinning when Dannel glanced sharply at him. "What?"

"Nothing."

On the short walk from where they parked to the police station, Dannel considered their options. Walk in and ask for Haider? He'd see them coming a mile away.

He'd probably see them coming a mile away no matter what they did.

It was tempting to simply go home and enjoy the doughnuts. But then Dannel remembered his brother's suspension from the force. The job Roland had always wanted to do.

Someone had attempted to sandbag his brother. Dannel wanted answers. He felt like they had too many loose threads needing to be tied together.

He couldn't help feeling that they were running out of time to knot them.

"Quid for your thoughts?" Chris nudged him lightly with his elbow.

"Thinking about Barnaby Sharrow's murder and everything else." Dannel waved his hands, unsure of how to voice his thoughts fully.

"We're about to have something else to ponder." Chris pointed to two familiar figures exiting the police station. "Hello, Detectives. Fancy running into you here."

"Yes, fancy meeting detectives outside a police station filled with them." DI Powell rolled her eyes at them. She waved her hand when Chris held the box of doughnuts out to them. "I'll pass."

"I won't." Haider grabbed one of the doughnuts for himself. "We can't tell you anything about the Sharrow case with or without a bribe."

"Can we..." Dannel trailed off.

Leaving Chris to distract the other detective, Dannel led Haider further down the pavement to the narrow passage leading toward the car park behind the police station. Dannel stared at the doughnut in Haider's hand. He suddenly forgot the questions he'd practised in his head.

"Dannel?" Haider brushed crumbs off his sleeve. "How can I help?"

"My brother." Dannel cursed his sudden loss of words.

"Roland?" Haider shifted the doughnut to his other hand. He stepped closer to Dannel. "He's been placed on temporary suspension pending an investigation."

"For what?"

Haider massaged his forehead, sighing heavily. "You and your fiancé will be the death of me."

"Not literally."

"Death of my career." Haider chuckled. "Off the record?"

"I don't have a record."

"Right." Haider took a bite of the doughnut and seemed to consider his words carefully. "Tampering with evidence in an ongoing investigation."

"Rolly?" Dannel knew his brother would never

have done anything to jeopardise a case. "Seriously? Rolly?"

"I happen to agree with you." Haider tilted his head around, checking for anyone passing by. "I've seen zero evidence. It's my case, and I'd certainly know if he had been."

"Which means?"

"He—or you and Osian—has managed to ruffle some important feathers." Haider popped the last bite of the doughnut into his mouth. "I've told you both repeatedly to let the police handle the investigation. There are a lot of toes you don't know not to step on here."

Dannel stared at him, mildly confused. "What?"

"Be careful. That's all I'm saying." Haider patted his shoulder, then headed back over to his partner.

So who is it?

The handsy judge, the not grieving widow, the solicitor who had Wayne's keys, or the angry bodyguard?

Handsy hamster in the courthouse with a silk tie?

Dannel had a distinct feeling it was going to get worse before it got better.

If it gets better.

SEVENTEEN
OSIAN

"Flowers? We need flowers."

This is societally sanctioned torture.

The three most important women in his life, barring Abra, had been chatting for two hours about flowers, menus, and venues. Olivia kept glancing over at him with a twinkle in her eyes. She was enjoying seeing her brother in the hot seat.

She'd basically dropped a few ideas into the ether and watched the chaos of his mum and mum-in-law-to-be with glee. Osian had hoped for a bit of help from her. But, unfortunately, she'd had no interest in reining them in thus far.

We are one hundred percent eloping. Hurt feelings be damned. I'm not putting Dannel through all this chaos; he'll never make it down the aisle.

"We do not, I repeat, do not need a full orchestra for anything connected to this wedding." Osian set his glass down harder than intended. He smiled apologetically at his sister for the wine dripping off the table. "Mum. Seriously. We're not interested in all this fuss."

"Sweetheart." His mum smiled mischievously at him. "You might want to remember to breathe. I wouldn't want you to hyperventilate before the wedding even happens."

"Are you all quite finished taking the mickey out of me?" Osian complained while they laughed. "How about we compromise? I'm tired of your experiment with reverse psychology."

"We would never." Dannel's mum feigned offence remarkably well. "The audacity of young people."

"Hilarious." Osian stretched his leg out to kick his snickering sister in the shin. "You can't convince me to agree to your real plan by terrifying me with all of this."

"Can't we?"

"How about this? We'll get married at the register office, then you can throw a hell of a party for us afterwards." Osian drained what little was left of the wine in his glass. "Princess Olivia can plan it for us."

"Excellent." Olivia rubbed her hands together with a wicked grin. "I'm seeing unicorns. And glitter. All things sparkly."

"You're not, actually." He decided it was time to make a hasty retreat. He got up, kissed them all on the cheek, and then raced for the door. "Lovely to see you all. Must run."

Leaving the cackling trio at Olivia's table, Osian fled his sister's home. They were exhausting. He'd almost prefer trying to solve a murder.

Almost.

With a dramatic sigh of relief, Osian decided to check on Dannel. A quick text conversation led to him changing directions. Dannel and Chris had gone over to the latter's workplace to do research.

And by research, Osian assumed they were digging into the lives of their suspects. Legally. Completely legally. He didn't think Chris would push the envelope too much.

Then again, Chris did have access to systems they didn't. He also had motivation in the form of a younger sister who'd been threatened by one of the suspects on their list. So worry was definitely a strong motivator.

The tube ride over to Chris's workplace gave Osian enough time to clear out his emails. He also outlined their next podcast script. They planned for one more episode before taking a break for the rest of the year.

"No pizza?" Chris greeted him once he'd stepped into office. "Follow me. We're back here."

"So, what have you found?" Osian stepped up behind Dannel's chair, wrapping his arms around him. "Anything interesting?"

"People share far too much information on social media." Chris slid across the office on his wheeled chair. He sidled up next to Dannel. "Several of the people who went out that night shared photos and videos."

"And?" Osian dragged a third chair over to sit behind them, resting his chin on Dannel's shoulder. "Did you learn anything new?"

"Satish Misra made loads of angry reviews on Barnaby and Wayne. He's definitely a disgruntled client." Chris switched browser tabs and highlighted a few. "Unethical. Failed to do the bare minimum. Avoid at all costs unless you want to lose your case. And those are the mild ones without swearing and threats."

"He's definitely got a motive then." Osian

wondered how difficult it would be to track the man down. "We should ask Wayne about him. What else did you discover?"

"Willa was surprisingly quiet on Instagram the night of the murder. She usually posts frequently on nights out, from a cursory look at her account." Chris scrolled through the page. "Interesting enough, though, one of Hamnet Allsop's daughters happened to be at the same pub, which might explain Edgar's presence."

"Did he go there with Willa?" Osian asked.

"Nope." Dannel tilted his head to rest against Osian's. "Not according to office gossip. They got close after a few drinks."

"Ah yes, the honest truth of office gossip." Osian knew from Wayne that nothing stayed a secret long amongst solicitors. "It doesn't really prove anything, whether or not they went together or decided to hook up there."

Shifting closer with his arm still wrapped around Dannel, Osian watched one of the short videos on Instagram. The camera panned around the room, showing the group of friends with beers. It zoomed in on someone having what appeared to be a heated conversation with both Barnaby and Wayne.

"Who's that?"

"No idea. It's the only video on her account, and it ends before you get a glimpse of their face." Chris switched to yet another tab on the browser. "I'm hazarding a guess it's Satish Misra."

"Can we prove it?" Osian asked.

"Maybe. I'll be right back." Chris headed out of the room.

"How'd the wedding planning go?" Dannel shifted around in the chair toward Osian. "Are we running away?"

"Forever?"

"I mean, they'd find us eventually." Dannel bent forward until their lips met. He grinned into the kiss. "You're probably worth the trouble."

"Quit snogging in my office." Chris slipped back inside. "Wayne and Roland are coming over. They're bringing food."

"And beer?"

"Just food. Despite appearances, I am working." Chris went over to a cabinet in the corner, opening one of the drawers. "We should try to find more on Satish Misra. And maybe chase down Handsy Hamster's daughter."

"Wayne can help with the former. I'll message Abs. She might know about the judge's daughter."

Osian wasn't sure any of what they had was actually helpful.

Chris held up several iPads he'd retrieved. "We need to trawl through the social media of everyone we know was at the pub that night. Then, with luck, we can create a timeline for who left and when. Plus, maybe we'll find more footage."

"Not a bad plan." Dannel grabbed one of the tablets while Chris returned to his computer. "I'll check to see if anyone else made complaints online about Barnaby Sharrow. Misra might not be the only client with an axe to grind."

"A client with access to Wayne's tie and car keys?" Osian reached for one of the iPads as well. "There was definitely more than one person involved in this murder. Has to be. And what about Edgar? He's not on social media."

"True. He might be in the background of someone else's video or photo." Chris checked his watch. "We've got maybe two hours before some of my co-workers return from their surveillance job."

"Plenty of time for a good snog," Osian teased.

"No, keep your lips to yourselves. I don't need a front-row seat to your romance. I'm already going to the wedding." Chris glared pointedly at both Osian and Dannel. "We need to pin down where Edgar went after leaving Willa's."

"How?" Dannel pushed Osian out of his face when he went in for another kiss. "Focus."

"I am." Osian settled back in his seat. "Is there any possible way to gain access to CCTV around Wayne's building? Anything to see Edgar or anyone else leaving?"

"Nope. The cameras were either off or turned in another direction." Chris paused when his phone rang. "Hang on."

They sat in relative silence while Chris stepped out to take a call. Dannel returned to attempting to find more videos from the night at the pub. Osian wondered if they could expand their search.

Wayne had given them a list of names of people at the pub. Of course, those were only the ones he remembered. Had other people attended? Osian decided to go through their followers, attempting to find anyone who'd gone.

"If I have to listen to one more drunken rendition of 'Bohemian Rhapsody.'" Dannel groaned. "Why do people enjoy karaoke so much?"

"You sing all the lines to *Hamilton* whenever we're listening to the cast album." Osian shifted his legs out of the way to avoid the kick aimed in his direction. "Hey. Check this out."

Dannel leaned across the table. "More singing?"

"No." Osian played the slightly blurry video, drawing Dannel's attention to the dark corner behind the couple entering the pub. "Wayne drapes his coat across a chair, then drops his tie on top. Anyone could've grabbed it."

The video certainly wasn't a smoking gun. However, it did offer a lead to follow. *Can we find footage of someone stealing the tie? Or at least of it vanishing from the pub?*

"It doesn't prove anything." Dannel went back to his own search. "Nothing concrete."

"True, but we have a starting point. It also gives us the exact time they arrived at the pub." Osian made sure to send the link to Chris. He might be able to clean up the footage. "More than we had. Maybe more than the police have."

But not enough to clear Wayne.

Not yet.

EIGHTEEN
DANNEL

SEARCHING THROUGH STRANGERS' SOCIAL MEDIA accounts was possibly the most boring thing Dannel had done in ages. He didn't understand the draw of posting every moment of one's life online. However, it did make snooping easier.

Perhaps another reason to avoid social media.

"Of all the sodding...."

Dannel dropped the iPad and watched Osian slam his phone on the table in a rare show of temper. "Ossie?"

"Drystan's been suspended."

"Drystan?" Dannel couldn't have been more shocked if Osian claimed the sky was neon green. "Drystan Rees. Your brother-in-law. Straightest arrow in the world? Dedicated his whole life to saving lives? Him? Suspended for what? I feel like we've had this conversation already."

"No clue. My sister just messaged me." Osian dropped into the chair. "He apparently called her to let her know."

"First Rolly? Then Drystan?" Dannel hated to feel paranoid, but it seemed more than a coincidence. "I'd say we've managed to get someone's attention."

"Judge Abbey did warn us about stepping on toes." Osian slouched down in the chair with a tired groan. "What kind of Pandora's box have we opened up?"

"Pandora's?" Dannel didn't think there were multiple kinds of a mythological box. "You were being figurative."

"I was being something." Osian stretched his arm out to grab his phone. "Well, it's too late to back out now, isn't it?"

"Probably."

Their silence together was usually comforting for Dannel. He'd always appreciated Osian's acceptance of his need for companionable quiet. Unfortunately, this time it felt oppressive.

The weight of worry settled heavily over both of them. They'd seen people with privilege and wealth abuse their power and get away with it. Dannel had no doubts two suspensions and a murder could simply be the tip of the iceberg.

Dannel stared off into the distance for several minutes before voices drew his attention to the doorway. "I smell Nando's."

"Chicken and chips? Best way to... What's wrong?" Roland asked, leading the way into the room. He dropped the bags in his arms on the table and crouched by his brother. "Dannel?"

"I'm fine." He waved off his brother's concern. "Drystan was suspended from the fire services, pending investigation."

"Investigation into what?" Roland helped Chris unload the collection of sodas he'd gotten from the office breakroom.

"Who knows? What are they investigating you for? They refused to give him any details. Sound familiar?" Osian still sat slumped in his seat, glowering at his mobile. "I'm waiting for Olivia to message me with details. Asking Abs to check in with her godmother and her judge friend."

"Chief Wilson might know." Dannel hadn't spoken with his old mentor at the fire station in a couple of weeks. "I can go by the station to have a chat with him."

"I can drive you when we're done eating," Roland offered readily. "We can leave these three to keep trying to dig through the cesspool of social media."

"Says the man who has a TikTok account." Osian sat up and dug through the bags to find a packet of chips. "The good news is, we don't know anyone else who can possibly be suspended or fired from the emergency services."

Over chicken and chips, they watched and rewatched various videos culled from Instagram and TikTok. Dannel felt a headache brewing, and the images began to blur together. It didn't help that he couldn't get his mind off Roland and Drystan's suspensions.

If we're being threatened, what's happening in the actual police investigation?

Could Haider have been bribed or threatened away from investigating anyone other than Wayne?

It was implausible yet still possible. Even the incorruptible had a price. Dannel wondered if Roland would mind swinging by the police station on their way to see Chief Wilson.

Haider might be willing to chat with him. The murderer had come for his little brother. Dannel intended to find out who it was.

After finishing up their late lunch, Dannel convinced Roland to leave with him. Chris wanted to take another shot at Edgar. Osian and Wayne decided to revisit Mrs Rose in the hopes she might have more information for them.

A long shot, but they had few options.

"Rolly?"

"Hmm?" He paused to glance over at Dannel before easing into traffic.

"I want to see if I can have a chat with Haider before we head to the fire station." Dannel hadn't wanted to tell Osian, who would probably insist on being the one to chat with the detective inspectors.

Despite his brother's attempts, Dannel refused to answer questions. He was too busy running through conversations in his head. He didn't want to lose his words, not when things had begun to heat up.

"Why are we stopping here first?" Roland found a parking spot across from the police station. "Dannel?"

"Just wait here for me. This won't take long." Dannel sent a quick text to Haider, asking him to meet outside, then walked across to sit on one of the benches not far from the entrance.

Haider took a seat beside him a few minutes

later. "I'm surprised to see you again so soon. Osian's usually the one wanting to talk."

"My brother and now my brother-in-law have been suspended within days of each other." Dannel waited for a couple to stroll by hand in hand before continuing. "There's this Rolls-Royce following us around. And some muscled-up private security tosser keeps making veiled threats like we're in a B-grade movie."

"Dannel."

"Wayne's not a murderer," Dannel insisted firmly. "And someone's going out of their way to make sure we stop trying to prove he isn't. And we—"

"Dannel," Haider repeated, cutting him off. "I need you to breathe for me."

"I am." Dannel wasn't sure how he'd missed the signs of a meltdown. "I am?"

"Think Harry Kane's going to win the golden boot for Chelsea?"

"Wrong team." Dannel blinked at the sudden change of conversation. "He's in with a shot."

"What team is it? Liverpool?"

"Tottenham. You can't be this clueless." Dannel found his breathing beginning to return to normal.

"I'm okay. Please stop assaulting my brain with your lack of football knowledge."

"How about you tell me why you're here?"

"I know you can't share details about the case." Dannel shifted uncomfortably on the bench.

"And you would be correct."

"But don't you find the entire case too convenient and odd?" Dannel wasn't even sure the sentence made sense in his own head, let alone spoken aloud. "I mean—"

"I do," Haider interrupted.

"Well?"

"I can't share details about an ongoing murder inquiry, particularly with a friend of one of our suspects." Haider tucked his hands into his pockets, leaning back against the bench. "Hypothetically, I can confirm all of this very odd."

"Hypothetically." Dannel watched several constables wander out of the station. "Has anyone discouraged you from looking too deeply beyond Wayne?"

"Leave it, Dannel." Haider got to his feet. He stared down at him for a moment. "I don't want to see you and Osian in a life or death situation again. Let me handle this investigation. It's my job. And I'm good at it."

"What if someone doesn't want you to do your job?"

"Leave it alone."

Conversation over, apparently.

Haider jogged up the steps to the station and disappeared inside. Dannel had no idea what his reaction meant. He wished Osian had been there for the brief chat, if only to decipher it for him.

Missing verbal and facial cues was such a pain.

"Well?" Roland prompted when Dannel got back into the vehicle.

"Haider agrees, hypothetically, things are odd." Dannel threw his hands up in the air and sighed in frustration. "No idea what exactly he means by it."

"I imagine he's getting pressure to close his case and make an arrest." Roland started the vehicle. "On to the fire station?"

"Maybe the chief will be less enigmatically confusing." Dannel trusted his former fire chief to be honest with him.

Early evening traffic made the short distance to the fire station take forever. Dannel tuned out his brother's frustrated cursing at the skills of the drivers around them. He texted Osian to see if they'd uncovered anything of use.

They hadn't. No smoking gun in the many

blurry videos. The most they'd proven was Wayne hadn't worn his tie out of the pub.

"Ortea. What are you doing here?"

"Making sure you still know how to prep your gear." Dannel didn't miss the stress of the work, but he did miss his fellow firefighters. They were a good bunch. "Chief in his office?"

"Come by the kitchen when you're done. Jess's husband brought dinner for us." He disappeared into the locker room, leaving Dannel to make his way further into the station.

"Dannel? Good to see you." Chief Wilson welcomed him into the office when he knocked on the open door. "It's been a while."

"Drystan Rees." Dannel stayed standing by the door. He wasn't sure how this conversation would go, since Haider had shut theirs down fairly quickly.

"You heard?" Chief Wilson motioned toward the chair. "Have a seat. I'm surprised Osian isn't here with you."

"What happened to Drystan?"

"Not my station."

"You can't tell me chiefs don't gossip." Dannel knew better. "Drystan's a good man. You know it. There's no way he'd jeopardise his family or career.

179

Yet somehow he's suspended pending investigation? And no one knows what for?"

"Son." Chief Wilson held a hand up to stop him from continuing. "What have you stepped into?"

"Think we might've stepped on a few toes." Dannel dropped into the seat across from Chief Wilson. "Important ones."

"Important toes?" Chief Wilson's lips twitched slightly. "Does this have anything to do with a dead barrister and your solicitor friend being questioned?"

Dannel shrugged.

"His chief was as surprised as I was." He tapped his fingers against the desk. "Strange. A firefighter being investigated, yet no one around him had any idea."

"Strange," Dannel agreed.

"Leave it with me, okay? I'll make a few calls. See if I can't find something out." Chief Wilson stood up, motioning for Dannel to follow. "Now, how go the wedding plans?"

"Don't ask."

"Am I still invited?"

"You're family." Dannel might have made progress with his relationship with his father, but the chief had a special place in their lives.

With no other things to follow, Dannel told

Roland to drop him off at home. He found Osian already there, doing research for their next podcast episode while watching the latest *Critical Role* episode. They were a few days out from needing to record.

"Ice cream?" Dannel wandered over to find the tub Evie had left behind on her last visit. "We can split it."

Grabbing the tub and a spoon, Dannel collapsed onto the couch. Osian grinned when he offered him the first spoonful. *True love is the first and last bite.* Dannel quickly filled him in on both conversations from earlier.

"Strange? Odd? Did anyone have anything useful to offer?" Osian offered Dannel the tub of ice cream. "Though, I'm surprised Haider gave you any sort of answer."

"Hypothetical." Dannel repeated the word a few times. "Hypothetical."

"Fancy way of getting around admitting to telling the truth." Osian bent forward to give Dannel a kiss. It tasted of coffee and caramel. "Think Chief Wilson will dig into Drystan being suspended?"

"Probably. He's always hated injustice of any kind." Dannel handed over the tub. "I'm more interested in Haider's response. I wish you'd been there to see his face. I can't place the expression."

"Why don't I get up early for a jog?"

"A jog by the police station?"

"It's on the way." Osian grinned.

"It's only on the way if you're intending to go to the police station."

NINETEEN
OSIAN

"If I didn't know you, I'd think I was being stalked." Haider barely even batted an eyelid when he spotted Osian jogging by him. "Can't I even get coffee and a doughnut in peace?"

His early morning patience had paid off. Osian had left before the sun came up, knowing Haider usually grabbed breakfast and walked to the station. It was his way of preparing himself for a long day of work.

"Completely unintentional."

"First, you don't jog. You walk. Second, you never walk this direction or this early in the morning." Haider took a bite of his doughnut. "Are you planning to pretend to stretch now? Keep jogging in place like you weren't waiting for me."

"Hypothetically speaking—"

"I'm having a distinct feeling of déjà vu." He finished up the last bite of his breakfast. "If I get indigestion, I'm blaming you."

"Hypothetically speaking—"

"No," Haider interrupted for a second time. "Have you considered your poking around in my investigation might be distracting me from solving a murder?"

"We're friends, right?" Osian paused to make sure he wasn't going to be cut off mid-sentence for the third time. "Nothing wrong with a cordial conversation between mates."

"Chatting about the weather and football is cordial conversation." Haider sipped his coffee and wandered over to sit on the steps leading up to a closed shop. "You want to tell me why you're tracking me down at half-six in the morning?"

In retrospect, coffee, as opposed to jogging, would've been a better way to start his morning. Osian went over to join Haider on the stairs. He carefully considered his options for a conversation starter.

"Dannel thought you seemed a little off last night. He was worried."

"He didn't." Haider raised an eyebrow at him

before taking another drink of his coffee. "You'd make a lousy interrogator. No poker face. Why don't you ask me straight up?"

"Has someone warned you off investigating Judge Allsop?" Osian admired the detective inspector's ability to not even flinch at the question. "Or maybe Edgar Smith?"

"Judge Allsop? Why bring him up?"

"Hamnet Allsop frequently bed-hopped, including with the deceased's wife." Osian took his phone out of his pocket and pulled out the still image from one of the videos they'd found. "His daughter at the pub the night of the murder. We found a video of Wayne leaving his jacket and tie within easy reach of at least twenty people."

"Osian." Haider set his coffee on the step between them. He grabbed Osian's phone, zooming in on the image. "None of this proves he's innocent."

"Reasonable doubt?"

"Reasonable doubt isn't my job. I'm a detective inspector, not a prosecutor." Haider went to hand the phone back. Instead, Osian scrolled to another video, one from the building showing someone leaving in Wayne's vehicle. "What am I watching? Where the hell did you get this?"

"That's not Wayne. You and I both know it.

Whoever this is, they're taller. They had his keys. They left and returned." Osian stretched his arms over his head in an attempt to release some of the tension in his back. "Listen. Someone took his tie and his car keys. Someone left a body in his boot."

"I know."

Osian stared in surprise at Haider, who chuckled. "Bastard. Are you enjoying our floundering around trying to convince you?"

"Immensely. Best entertainment I've had since this case started." Haider lifted his cup of coffee up in a mock salute. "I can't close the case against Dankworth."

"Why?"

"Don't pout at me. I'm not your fiancé." Haider handed Osian's phone to him. "If we close the case on Wayne, the murderer knows we're onto them."

"Have we made your life difficult?"

"When don't you?" Haider offered a wry smile. "Since you can't seem to help yourselves and nothing I say will change your minds, could you two at least try to be careful? And try not to bugger up my case so badly that I can't solve it?"

"We'll do our best."

"Osian?"

"What?"

"In my experience, things always get worse before they get better in an investigation involving people like them." Haider got to his feet, nodded at Osian, and walked off whistling to himself.

As warnings went, Haider's had felt fairly ominous yet mild-mannered. They had murder and two suspensions. How much worse could it get?

On the plus side, Osian was relieved to know Haider believed in Wayne's innocence. He ignored the slight twinge of guilt for pressing their detective friend for answers. *Things always get worse before they get better.*

The words echoed around Osian's brain when he rounded the corner to find the Ortea shop closed. Dannel paced outside with his uncle and auntie watching him. They were obviously attempting to calm him down.

Unsuccessfully.

"Ossie." Dannel rushed over to him, throwing his strong arms around Osian and crushing him in an embrace. "They're inspecting the shop after some supposed tip."

"A tip about what?"

"Illegal activity is all I could get out of the police who showed up twenty minutes ago." Dannel's uncle stepped up behind them. He rested a hand on his nephew's shoulder. "It's going to be okay. We're heading home. Nothing to do here. I'll call you."

Dannel nodded to his uncle and focused on Osian. "I saw Edgar Smith across the street in the Rolls-Royce."

"Are you sure?"

"He had the window down." Dannel's fingers gripped the back of Osian's shirt. "Tosser winked at me before driving off. He wanted me to see him."

"I'm calling Chris." Osian kept one arm around Dannel while reaching into his pocket for his phone. "And maybe Abra. I think it's time we pay her godmum's friend another visit."

"Ossie."

"We can sit back on the defence trying to keep the ball out of the net." Osian managed to unlock his phone with his thumb. Dannel didn't seem ready to step back. "We're allowing ourselves to be pushed so far back we might as well make an own goal."

"Ah, football. Attractive virile men in shorts." Ian strolled over to them, casually flicking his scarf over his shoulder. "A beautiful sport. Is everything all right, darlings?"

"Fine," Dannel muttered.

"Not exactly fine," Osian countered immediately. "We've found ourselves in a…"

"Quagmire?" Ian smiled brilliantly while offering the perfect word when Osian floundered. "Why don't you come up to my flat for a coffee? I can share the little rumours I've heard recently."

"Ian."

"Come along, darlings." Ian turned back toward the building.

Leading the way inside to his flat, Ian pushed them to sit on his plush leather sofa. He busied himself in the kitchen making tea with a dash of gin. His home always reminded Osian of 1920s movie opulence.

Glitz, glamour, and wealth.

Ian sat across from them with his long coat and scarf draped over the back of the chair. He gestured imperiously for them to begin. Osian had to chuckle for a moment before starting the tale.

"Well, well, well, you are in a spot of bother, darlings, aren't you?" Ian sipped his tea slowly. He gently set the cup down on a saucer. "Hamnet Allsop. Allsop. I knew an Allsop. Second cousin, I believe. A pretty thing. A mildly talented stage actor, a few years younger than me. We had a wild fling in the '80s."

"Did you?" Osian grinned at Ian while Dannel

nudged him with his elbow. "What? Aren't you curious?"

"No," Dannel muttered into his tea. "Fine. Maybe."

"Who could resist Ian's charms?" Osian winked at him.

"My point, young Osian, is you've trampled all over the sensitive egos of the untouchable." Ian lifted up his teacup again. He paused before taking a drink. "You know, I've an invite to a charity gala tonight. All to benefit the theatre. And I've left it dreadfully late to find my plus one. Either of you up for wining, dining, and a side dish of intrigue?"

Dannel immediately held his hands up. "Not it."

Cinderella is going to the ball.

Scrounging around in their wardrobe later that evening, Osian found his old suit from a friend's wedding years ago. Thankfully, it still fit him perfectly. Unfortunately, he hated the way the collar of the jacket made his neck itch.

It was the main reason the suit had been consigned to the farthest corner of their wardrobe. He occasionally pulled it out for a date. Dannel had a fondness for him in it.

Like now.

"Enjoying the view?" Osian watched Dannel in

the mirror while adjusting his bow tie. "You could always come with us."

"No," Dannel responded instantly. "I will miss dancing with you, though."

"Come on, then." Osian turned around and held a hand out. "We've plenty of time for a dance or two before the pumpkin carriage arrives."

"Sounds messy. Is Ian your fairy godmother then?"

"Pretty sure he'd claim to be the wicked step-mother." Osian caught Dannel's hand and dragged him into an awkward half-turn. They both wound up bumping against the side of the bed. "She had the best outfits."

"Did she? Pretty sure I can whip up a fairy godmother cosplay for you," Dannel laughed.

They spun in a slow circle in their bedroom. Osian enjoyed their quiet moment together. It was a much-needed fortification to prepare for the evening ahead.

Closing his eyes, he briefly rested his forehead against Dannel's shoulder. They weren't dancing so much as twisting slowly in a tight embrace. Dannel's muscular arms tightened around him.

"I could say something romantic," Dannel commented absently.

"But?"

"I've got nothing, and you just trod on my toe." Dannel hopped around on one foot, scowling at Osian. "Laugh it up. You're going to spend all evening with an itchy collar while I eat pizza and play *Mass Effect*."

"Rude."

An hour later, Osian was walking into the charity gala, already having second thoughts. He didn't fancy spending an evening mired in a mine-field of small talk. Times like these gave him a greater appreciation for Dannel's need for quiet.

A parade of the rich, the famous, and wannabes swarmed around them. Famous (and infamous) figures from the London theatre scene mingled amongst the generous donors. Ian fit right in with all of them.

Osian did not.

No matter how well his suit fit him.

"Come along, darling." Ian swept over with two flutes of champagne, offering one to Osian. He rested a hand on his arm. "Let's set our whirling dervish into motion, shall we? I've seen our target across the room."

Ian paused to say hello here and there; it took them ten minutes to catch up to the judge and his wife. Osian was almost surprised to see them there as a couple. All the rumours made it seem as if they could barely stand one another.

"Hamnet." Ian sounded so frosty Osian half-expected icicles to drip from his voice.

"Barrett." Judge Allsop's sneer morphed into a smile when his wife approached Ian with a kiss to the cheek. "It's been a long time since you graced us with your presence."

Ian waited until the judge's wife had moved on, then stepped in close. "And you've been such a naughty boy, flexing your power like a small child playing with toy soldiers. Small-minded men, darling, always need to be so careful with their relationships and reputations. One badly thrown stone can send everything crashing down."

"At least I have power."

"I've never been just a pretty face." Ian flicked a speck of nothing off his sleeve. "Now, why don't you cease your attempts at ruining people's lives and focus on your own. Oh, and Hamnet?"

"What?" he hissed, keeping his voice low as his wife stepped back over.

"You will tell your mother I said hello, won't you? I haven't seen her in ages." Ian patted the judge on the sleeve with an air of condescension. "I simply must catch up with her. I've so much news to share."

Osian waited until they were out of hearing range to burst out laughing. "Can I be you when I grow up?"

"If you're very, very lucky."

TWENTY

DANNEL

"Right. So..." Dannel's gaze shifted from Osian to Drystan then back to his fiancé. "Did I hit my head in the middle of the night? Or, are you seriously telling me our Ian successfully cowed the big bad wolf into submission?"

"Now, there's an odd sentence I bet you never thought you'd utter. Or, udder?" Osian grinned when Dannel groaned at his joke. "Drystan popped by with coffee and pastries. He's been reinstated. The investigation has magically resolved itself."

Wandering over to grab one of the coffees, Dannel sank into the couch. He grimaced at the first taste, causing Osian to laugh again. They traded cups.

Ah, much better.

"Any word on Rolly?" Dannel caught his phone when Osian tossed it to him. He had several missed messages from his uncle, mum, and brother. "Oh, here we go. He's waiting for word from his supervisor. Mum says they're allowed to open the shop today. No idea how or why. Inspector cancelled their visit scheduled for tomorrow."

"Convenient. Odd, but convenient." Drystan grabbed one of the pastries from the box. "All this because Ian made a few veiled comments at a charity gala?"

"If Chris's James Bond, Ian's gotta be M." Osian dunked his pastry into his coffee then took a bite.

"An eccentric M." Drystan wandered over to sit on the arm of the sofa. "Then again, anyone who goes by a letter of the alphabet instead of a name is unconventional at best."

Making his way into the kitchen, Dannel hunted around in the fridge for the milk. He topped off his coffee, swirling the cup to mix it. Another taste had him adding a little more.

Perfect.

While Osian recapped his evening out for Drystan, Dannel finished reading his messages. He found one from Evie wanting to go for a run. She suggested meeting downstairs in an hour.

She had news.

News?

An hour later, Dannel left the brothers-in-law still chatting over their pastries. He jogged down the stairs out of the building to find Evie already waiting. She zipped up her hoodie and followed his lead toward the nearby park where they frequently ran when the weather worked out.

"Chief Wilson pulled me into his office yesterday." Evie waited until they'd fallen into a comfortable pace on the path to speak. "An anonymous complaint was filed against me. And then, just as quickly, it disappeared."

"Did it?"

"He also mentioned your visit and Drystan's suspension." Evie fell behind him to avoid a dog walker on the path, then caught back up to him. "Though, when I saw your uncle this morning, he said Drystan had been reinstated. Are we just a revolving door of oddness?"

"Have we ever been anything other than a revolving door of oddness?" Dannel went left at a fork in the path. "I've a feeling Ian may have simply redirected our problems, not solved them."

"Pessimist."

"Optimistic realist," Dannel retorted.

They ran in silence for a circuit around the park. Dannel's mind went to all the possible worst-case scenarios. Spiralling, his mum always called it.

Dannel preferred to think of it as following a path to the worst possible conclusion. If he could process and handle that, everything else was easy. It helped him cope.

"Pop by the gym for a workout?" Evie jogged in place when they finished their fourth circuit. "I haven't done weights in a while."

"Not today." Dannel wanted to get home and check in on his uncle and auntie. "Maybe tomorrow? It's been too long."

Walking another half circuit, Dannel stretched his legs out before heading home. He was happy to find his auntie Myriam already in the shop. She waved him inside with a bright smile.

"Your uncle and mum are in the back, making sure the inspector didn't bugger up the inventory." She offered him a little cup of coffee from the fresh pot she'd made. "Your Osian left with Abra. Something about chatting up her godmum. And you, my dear, are in desperate need of a shower. You're stinking up the shop."

Before Dannel could defend himself, a knock on the glass door caught his attention. *Haider?* The detective inspector beckoned him to step outside. He gave his auntie a quick kiss on the cheek and grabbed a second cup of coffee for Haider.

"Morning. Coffee? My auntie makes it nice and strong." Dannel offered the cup to him. "What brings you to our neighbourhood?"

"What have you two done?" Haider followed Dannel into the building and up to their flat. "Seriously. What happened between the last time we spoke and now?"

"Ian?"

"Your eccentric neighbour with the theatre production company?"

"Who apparently has more connections than we thought." Dannel didn't know what to do once they'd gotten into the flat. He hesitated before going to sit on the sofa. *Am I supposed to tell him to have a seat? Why is he here?* "Don't you have a job to do?"

"I'm basking in the warmth of your welcome."

"I gave you coffee. My auntie's coffee. It's the best in the city." Dannel switched his cup from one hand to the other, then back again. "You're making me nervous. Why are you here?"

"I don't want to alarm you—"

"Too late," Dannel interrupted. "The police

showing up is usually cause for alarm even when it's my brother."

"He hasn't been reinstated." Haider didn't offer any further information, so Dannel waited him out. In his experience, non-autistics always struggled with silence, even the police. "We're going to make a few arrests."

"I am now alarmed."

"A show, if you will, to draw out the killer."

Dannel narrowed his eyes on the detective, who continued to lean against the closed front door. "Why are you telling me?"

"You and your fiancé have a tendency to make poor decisions when pressed." Haider sipped his coffee. "I'm trying to head off any potential problems to a perfectly executed plan."

"Name one poor decision," Dannel muttered indignantly.

"One ended up with your fiancé down a well."

"Not exactly Osian's fault." Dannel didn't think it was fair to blame either of them for the decisions made by a serial killer. "He was trying to rescue Ian."

"And now you're trying to rescue Wayne Dankworth." Haider crossed the room and sat across from Dannel. "The well this time might be deeper than you think. I'm not sure you'll survive the fall. Either of you."

"Who are you arresting?"

"More of a bringing in for questioning," Haider hedged.

Frowning at the detective inspector, Dannel got the distinct feeling he'd missed some subtext in their conversation. Where was Osian when he needed him? Haider continued to wait patiently while sipping his coffee.

"You're arresting Wayne."

"A show."

"You can keep saying it's a show, but the papers will run with the idea a solicitor has been arrested in the murder of a barrister." Dannel had no doubt the entire thing would turn into an absolute circus. "Who else?"

"Listen...."

"Who else?" Dannel repeated the question when Haider failed to continue. "Roland?"

"Again, merely a show to hopefully force the killer to make a mistake."

"A show that could ruin their careers? Do the police actually fake arrests?"

"Not an arrest. Technically." Haider shrugged casually.

Dannel set his cup to one side. He rubbed his hands against his knees, trying to ease the sudden rush of tension in his body. "Easy to be cavalier when it's not your life."

"We're on the same side."

"Are we?" Dannel got to his feet.

He knew Haider and Osian were friends. They attended a support group together. The detective inspector had become a mentor of sorts for Osian.

"I thought we were."

Dannel breathed out heavily and dropped down on the sofa again. "Mum says I hold grudges for too long."

"What have I done now? I haven't arrested you or Osian in ages," Haider teased. "Do you want to talk about it? Hypothetically?"

He is joking, right? I can never tell.

At least, Dannel assumed the man was teasing. Haider leaned forward with his elbows resting on his knees. He waited patiently for Dannel to speak.

"Hypothetically." Dannel sank into the cushions and scrubbed his fingers across his head in frustration. "I'm scared for my family. Who do you think killed Barnaby Sharrow?"

"I've theories." Haider tilted his coffee cup, then frowned. "None I intend to share with you."

"Then why are you here?"

"To make certain you don't do anything foolish." Haider carried the cup into the kitchen, rinsing it out and setting it in the sink. "The killer, whoever they might be, may have backed off slightly. It's time for you to allow me to do my job. I'd prefer to do so without the added stress of interference from true crime podcasters who have no sense of self-preservation."

"Harsh."

Having said his piece, Haider seemed ready to leave. Dannel closed the door behind him with a frustrated sigh. *Well, that was uninformative and confusing.*

After a long text to Osian about the surprise visit, Dannel channelled his nervous energy into painting googly eyes. The mindless task helped him process the conversation with Haider. He had hundreds to transform into rusty rivets.

Opening the window in their workshop to allow the breeze to clear out paint fumes, Dannel started in on the first one. His eyes started to blur after an hour of working on the tiny beads. In addition, he had a severe migraine brewing.

Googly eyes made the best rivets for armour. He had a new commission for a *Fallout* cosplay.

Painting them was going to be the most tedious part.

How's Haider's plan going to work? How is taking Wayne in going to force the killer into making a mistake? Why do I always think of the best questions after a conversation is over?

TWENTY-ONE
OSIAN

"WELL, THAT WAS A COLOSSAL WASTE OF OUR time." Osian followed Abra down the street from her godmum's place. She'd brushed them off while rushing into her vehicle and leaving for the airport. "She was mighty anxious to avoid chatting about the Allsops and Sharrows."

"Sounds like the bad plot to one of those Westerns my dad used to watch." Abra grabbed Osian's arm to yank him out of the way of a passing cyclist. "Listen, why don't we pop by Chris's office? See what he's up to?"

"Abra and Chris," Osian started in a sing-song tone.

"Shut it. There's no Abra and Chris." She shoved

him, only to yank him closer for a second time when a motorcycle hopped the kerb, heading straight for him. "What the—"

Stumbling against the sudden change of momentum, Osian caught Abra's hand and dragged her up a nearby flight of steps. He watched the motorcycle disappear around the corner. The rider had been decked out in black gear from head to toe, including a helmet completely covering their face. No number plate on the bike.

Is someone trying to kill me or scare me?

It can't have just been an accident.

You don't accidentally hop the kerb on a bike like that and narrowly miss running someone over.

"Oz? You okay?" Abra checked him over carefully. "Did he clip you?"

"No, I'm fine." Osian fumbled in his pocket for his phone. He sent a quick text to Chris, then hunted through his contact list for Haider's number and hit send. "Someone tried to run me over."

"Your greeting needs work." Haider was silent for a moment. Then, "Are you joking?"

"You heard me." Osian grabbed his phone tightly. "I'm sure there's CCTV footage of the incident."

"Osian."

"I didn't ask someone to run me over." Osian didn't appreciate the disbelief in Haider's voice. "I was minding my own business."

"Osian. You need to take a deep breath," Haider interrupted him. "Where are you?"

"Someone tried to run me down on the pavement. I'm on the pavement." Osian sat down heavily on the step when reality began to really sink in. "We're... bugger, I have no idea where we are."

"You literally live within a ten-minute jog from here. Give me the phone." Abra snapped her fingers in front of his face until he surrendered it to her. "Haider?"

While Abra filled Haider in on their location, Osian focused on breathing. He calmed his heart rate down, and slowly his hands stopped shaking. They'd obviously been followed.

The motorcycle attack seemed less finesse and more brute force. Not a calculated show of power. But who? Edgar Smith was the first name to come to mind.

"He said to stay here." Abra offered him back the phone.

"Okay." Osian stared blankly at her before

finally reaching up to take his phone. "You can head home if you want, Abs. Don't you have to work later?"

"Oz." She sat beside him and bumped her shoulder against his. "I'm not leaving you here on the steps alone to contemplate your mortality."

"I'm contemplating a nice long vacation." Osian shook his hands out, then rolled his shoulders a few times. "Remember when your body didn't hurt from a little tension?"

"Easy there, gramps." Abra laughed when he elbowed her in the side. "Want me to call Dannel?"

"Not yet."

To his surprise, Chris arrived before the police did. He got a few details from Osian, then promptly walked across the street into a shop. Abra seemed bemused by his sudden appearance.

"So, are you two not dating then?"

"Chris and me? We had a little fun."

"And?"

"Sometimes, Osian, adults have a little fun, and that's all they want. I believe the authorities have arrived." Abra nodded toward the approaching detective inspectors. "I think I'll pop across the street to join Chris. I've no doubt he's charming his way into getting hold of the CCTV footage before the police take it."

Osian watched her dart across the street, narrowly avoiding traffic, and had to chuckle. He turned his attention to the two detectives in front of him. "Before you start in about me not being careful, I was quite literally walking down the street minding my own business when some wanker drove onto the pavement."

"Is it possible this was an accident?" Detective Inspector Powell seemed as pleased to see Osian as she usually did.

"Possible? Sure." Osian pushed himself off the step, stood up and walked toward the detectives. He leaned against the railing for a moment. His legs were still a bit shaky. "As likely as my being knighted for services to cosplay kind."

"We're going to pull the CCTV footage. Is there anything useful you can tell us?" Haider reached out to place a hand on Osian's shoulder. "Are you okay?"

"Fine. Uninjured." Osian waved off the concern. "I can tell you loads of useless things. For example, I've listened to the *Hamilton* cast album over five hundred times."

"Osian." Haider massaged his temples for a few seconds. "Can you tell us anything about the rider?"

"They were on a motorcycle? One of the fancy, fast ones." Osian shook off the last bit of tension with a forced laugh. "I'm guessing a bloke from what I could see of their body underneath the riding gear. Dressed in all black down to the helmet. It was straight out of a movie."

"I'm going to see about the CCTV." DI Powell left Haider to deal with Osian.

"Something I said?"

"No. What about the person who attempted to run you over? Did they say anything?" Haider didn't rise to Osian's bait.

"Oh, yes, in the five seconds the entire event took, they had time for a full monologue." Osian raised his hand to stop Haider from speaking. "Sorry. I'm sorry. I'm a bit on edge."

"Sit." Haider pushed Osian down on the step and joined him. "You weren't hit?"

"No. I'm fine."

"You're not fine. You're shaky and telling worse jokes than usual." Haider checked his phone when it buzzed in his pocket. "Seems you've already had a visitor check in on you."

"Have I?" Osian responded with an angelic grin.

"Any reason for my partner to run into Chris Kirwin in the shop over there?" Haider continued to read whatever message DI Powell had sent to him. "Pure coincidence?"

"Maybe he fancied a packet of crisps?" Osian reached for his own phone when it beeped.

"Tell Kirwin to leave my investigation alone." Haider leaned over in a blatant attempt to read the message. "How many times do I have to warn you off? I don't want to wind up visiting you in the hospital again... or worse."

"Morbid." He tilted the screen away from Haider. "Have you ever attempted to tell Chris Kirwin anything? Besides, I didn't ask him to speed over here in an attempt to see if the mysterious rider might be Edgar Smith or someone connected to him."

"My job used to be so simple. I do not enjoy being part of an episode of *Scooby-Doo*," Haider complained.

"Am I Shaggy or Scooby?"

"Fred?"

"I can't decide if you're saying I'm pretty or dim." Osian glowered at Haider. "Listen, you know we're not trying to be difficult on purpose, right?"

"It just comes naturally."

Statement.

Not a question.

"Rude."

"I'm begging you to back off. Stop poking at bears. I'm better at handling them." Haider slowly got to his feet as DI Powell jogged across the street toward them. "I'm paid to do so."

TWENTY-TWO

DANNEL

Osian: Can you meet us at the café across from the park?

THE TEXT FROM OSIAN HAD SENT WARNING bells off in Dannel's mind. Not the words themselves; they were an innocuous invitation. He just couldn't shake the tendrils of fear spiking up his spine.

It reminded him too much of the night of Osian's last job as a paramedic.

There were nights when the call from Abra haunted his dreams. She'd handed her phone to Osian after begging Dannel to talk him out of his shock. He'd barely managed to get a whispered "hello."

You're being ridiculous. That was ages ago. Ossie's fine.

He'd planned to meet Osian at home later. Instead, the text made him feel edgy. Maybe the murder itself had him paranoid. Seeing Osian didn't do anything to assuage his worry.

His Osian had definitely experienced a shock. *Why's he look so lost?* Dannel immediately slipped into the seat beside him, barely acknowledging Chris's presence with a nod.

"Where's Abs?" Dannel tried to nudge Osian out of his silence.

"She had to get ready for work," Chris offered. "Why don't I get a round of tea for the three of us?"

"Ossie?"

"I'm okay." Osian met Dannel's wide-eyed stare and reached out to grab his hand. Their fingers intertwined, resting on Dannel's thigh. "Seriously, not a scratch on me."

"Yeah, but not every hurt leaves a physical mark." Dannel had seen Osian through the long nights dealing with his post-traumatic stress. "Are you sure?"

"Right as rain. A little almost collision with a motorcyclist won't keep me down for long." Osian squeezed his hand tightly. "Haider doesn't think they'll be able to identify the rider."

"But?"

"I'm 70 percent certain I know who it is." Chris reappeared, placing a plate of cakes on the table. "Tea'll be out in a second."

"Edgar Smith?"

"He's not foolish enough to involve too many people in whatever this is." Chris selected the largest of the cakes for himself. He grinned when Osian grumbled at him. "He's smart."

Dannel ignored both of them to focus on the vital question. "Foolish? How so?"

"The easiest way to keep a secret is to avoid sharing it."

"The easiest way to keep a secret is not to have one," Osian countered. He split the banoffee pie cake in half and offered the larger portion to Dannel. "Let's say, for argument's sake, Edgar's the killer. We've assumed someone put him up to it. What if he did it all on his own?"

"Why?" Chris wiped his fingers clean on a napkin, then grabbed his mug of tea. "No motive.

Edgar's capable of murder. I've no doubts. Not for the fun of it, though."

"He did threaten your sister." Osian glanced over at Dannel when he placed a hand on Osian's arm. "What?"

"Tact, Ossie. Tact." Dannel had to grin at the role reversal.

"You're not even half as funny as you think you are," Osian grumbled good-naturedly.

"What about the CCTV?" Dannel decided they needed to refocus. All the sugar and caffeine wasn't doing anything to help. "Anything on who tried to pancake Osian?"

"And I even shared the last half of cake with you." Osian flicked a chocolate flake at Dannel. "According to our own personal security officer, the footage showed nothing useful. Just some wanker on a fancy motorcycle."

Fancy wanker on a fancy motorcycle.

It sounded like the lines from a musical. Maybe not a first act song, but definitely somewhere in the second one. A dance number with a lot of chaos on the stage. Dannel could almost see the costumes and set in his mind.

"First of all, I am not anyone's personal security officer." Chris waved his spoon at Osian. "Second, I never claimed the CCTV footage was useless to me. I said the coppers won't find anything on it to identify their criminal."

"But?" Dannel prompted when Chris and Osian got into a brief duel with spoons. "Could you two pretend for all of five seconds you're grown adults?"

"I could take him."

Dannel silenced Osian with a glare, then turned expectantly to Chris. "You were saying?"

"The police don't know Edgar Smith. Didn't grow up with him. Didn't serve in the military with him." Chris dropped his spoon onto the table. He leaned back in his seat and folded his arms across his chest, sighing heavily. "It was him."

"So, how do we prove it? Any of it?" Osian asked the question on Dannel's mind. "I'm not entirely convinced Haider's going to be able to do anything aside from pulling Wayne in for question."

"Wayne and Roland," Chris corrected. "DI Powell mentioned it when I ran into her. They're picking them up this afternoon. I got the feeling they'd been delayed for some reason."

"I don't like it." Dannel gripped his mug of tea so tightly that Osian reached out to gently ease it out of his hand. "Sorry."

"Rolly's a big lad. He'll be okay." Osian linked

their fingers together, letting Dannel squeeze his hand. "Maybe he'll learn something from the detective inspector while he's there, pretending to be interrogated."

"It's all pretend until it's not," Chris muttered into his tea, ignoring the glare they both sent his way. "Haider's a decent bloke. Good police."

"But you think we need to see if we can find the evidence to prove Wayne's innocent because he might not be able to." Osian was obviously on the same wavelength as Chris, since the man immediately nodded.

Dannel didn't have the same level of confidence in their ability to stumble on the answers to this mystery. "Why would he try to run Ossie over?"

"He has a point. I'm charming and attractive." Osian winked at Dannel, who rolled his eyes. "What? I am. You're the one who wants to marry me."

"The idea is losing its lustre."

"Can we focus?" Chris snapped his fingers a few times in front of them. "I'd imagine since the subtle scare tactics haven't worked and you fought fire with Ian. They've now moved on to more..."

"Plebeian methods?" Dannel offered when Chris

struggled for a word. "Then again, murder involves getting your hands dirty."

"Not everyone with wealth and power is corrupt." Chris finished his tea, then shoved the mug toward the centre of the table. "You've both got a bit of a grudge towards their sort."

"Your sort, you mean?" Osian glanced at Dannel when he gently squeezed his hand. "What? I'm not being narky. Chris might've walked away from his family, but he grew up in the same circles."

"And not everyone in those circles is corrupt," Chris repeated himself.

"Give them time. Money and unchecked power are rarely conducive to creating kind, caring human beings." Osian made an excellent point, in Dannel's opinion. "Do I need to give you a list of people who've found themselves in one scandal or another when their privilege went to their heads?"

Deciding to disrupt the argument before it could get started, Dannel redirected the conversation to the most essential part. Edgar Smith. No matter who had a grudge against Barnaby Sharrow, he was obviously involved.

To Dannel, it seemed simple enough.

Find the connection to Edgar Smith, and they'd likely discover who'd wanted Barnaby and Wayne out of the picture. Dannel believed they knew who'd pulled the figurative trigger; now, they needed to determine who hired him.

How hard could it be?

"How do you draw Edgar Smith out?" Osian had sat in silence, sipping his tea for several minutes before finally deciding to stop prodding Chris. "You'd know him better than us. Chances of him talking?"

"Less than zero." Chris stood up, brushing crumbs off his shirt. "I'll swing by his flat. See if I can goad him into making a mistake."

"Want company?" Osian glanced over at Dannel, who shrugged and nodded after a second of thought. "We can come with you."

TWENTY-THREE

OSIAN

After a brief debate, Chris had caved into allowing them to ride with him across London. Edgar Smith had either done well for himself or used family money to afford his swanky home. Osian couldn't help his sharp whistle when they stood staring up at the renovated Regency-era home.

How much money was a private security guard making to afford a home in Regent's Crescent? They had to cost a good eight to ten million pounds. It had to be nice being able to rely on a family fortune.

Or had something more sinister provided the wealth required to allow him to live quite literally in the lap of luxury?

"How many millions do you think he sank into this place?" Dannel wondered. He leaned against the lamppost, watching Chris pace with his phone to his ear. "Ossie?"

"Hmm?"

"Stop trying to listen to his conversation." Dannel adjusted the headphones that he'd brought out of his backpack. All the traffic noise had put him on edge. The blissful cushioned silence helped. "What do you think?"

"About?"

"These places. Apartments. Flats. Whatever they want to call them. The estate agent's website doesn't list how much they go for." Dannel waved Osian over to show him what he'd found on his phone. "Not even a price range."

"If you have to ask the price, you probably can't afford it."

"If they listed the price, we still wouldn't be able to." Dannel pocketed his phone, then wrapped his arms around Osian when he leaned into his body. "Think about it; if my uncle didn't own the building, we'd never live where we do, and it's definitely cheaper than these places."

"Family money." Osian canted his head to one side to watch Chris wrap up his call. "What time is it in America? Maybe he's chatting with his sister."

"Rolly texted me earlier." Dannel reached a

hand up to adjust the level of noise cancellation on his headphones. "They apparently ruled out the client. They're still looking at Willa, though."

"What's her motive, though?"

"To be fair, she's seems more the type to make some sort of professional dig. File a complaint." Dannel knew people like Willa. He'd worked with a few at the fire department over the years. "She's not getting her hands dirty enough to get herself in any sort of legal trouble."

"True, though Haider would probably point out our gut instincts aren't evidence." Osian stepped out of his arms when Chris wandered back over. "Everything under control?"

"Tamsyn." Chris frowned at his phone. His fingers gripped so tightly that Osian wondered if the device was about to crack. "She thinks someone's following her."

"How can she tell?"

"She lives in a tiny little spot in Florida. She knows everyone in the town. Everyone. Strangers tend to stand out, especially ones with accents." Chris closed his eyes and breathed deeply for several seconds. He folded his arms across his chest. "I doubt he'd actually hurt her. Scare her and me, though? Definitely."

They were silent for a while. Then, finally, Chris scowled over his shoulder toward the opposite end of the crescent. Osian followed his gaze and spotted an intimidating figure closing the distance between them.

"Following me now?" Edgar stalked the last few steps until he stood almost toe-to-toe with Chris.

They were similar in their stature and held themselves almost identically as well. Likely their shared military experience. It reminded Osian of two dangerous predators sizing each other up.

"Pulled your motorcycle out of storage?" Chris threw the words at Edgar like daggers, clearly waiting for the man to flinch.

He didn't.

"Sold my motorcycle ages ago. Why? Has something happened?"

Exchanging a glance with Dannel, Osian caught him by the sleeve to pull him behind Chris. The two men obviously needed to engage in either a conversation or a fistfight. And whichever they chose, Osian had no intention of getting in the middle.

It was far more entertaining to watch from a distance.

I should not find this amusing. We're talking about murder and conspiracies. Murderous conspira-

cies. Oh, I like that. We're using it for a podcast episode.

"Ossie?" Dannel leaned over and whispered, "Not sure you should be grinning when I'm pretty sure Chris is about two seconds away from throwing a punch."

"Bugger," Osian muttered.

As amusing as the posturing was, Osian had no doubts Chris throwing a punch would only wind up causing trouble for him. Edgar had a gift for riling their friend up. Any physical altercation could be used against them.

"Since you're so interested in my movements." Edgar paused for a moment, obviously enjoying how irate Chris was becoming. Osian braced himself for whatever verbal bomb the man intended to drop. "I'll be leaving the country next week. Thought I'd do a bit of travelling. Get a bit of sun. London is so dreary this time of year, don't you think? I've always wanted to visit Florida."

Osian lunged forward immediately to grab Chris by the back of his jacket, stumbling slightly when it wasn't enough to halt the larger man's movement. "Easy, Chris."

"Maybe if you spent less time obsessing over what I'm doing, you'd see there's someone a little higher up with a closer connection to Sharrow's wife than I have." Edgar tapped his nose with his finger and smirked at Chris, who looked about five seconds away from punching the man. "Florida's lovely this time of year."

"Smarmy wanker," Dannel muttered.

Osian failed miserably in his attempt not to laugh. "Give me a hand? I feel like Spiderman trying to hold back the Hulk."

"Do you mind?" Edgar broke into Osian's debate with Dannel. "We're having a conversation."

"No, you're not having a conversation. You're being a massive pillock, hoping to goad Chris into making an arse of himself." Osian stared pointedly at Dannel, who rolled his eyes. He tried to lock his legs to keep Chris from moving toward Edgar. "He's dragging me forward like I'm a sodding toddler."

"And I'm supposed to help?" Dannel nudged Osian out of the way. He looped an arm around Chris's waist and walked him back. "Not quite the Hulk."

"For one, I'm not green." Chris deftly broke Dannel's hold on him. "I'm fine. I'm not going to touch the— Him. I'm not going to lay a hand on him and risk being arrested. Something I'm sure he wants."

"Am I not needed for this chat?" Edgar drew their attention back to him. "If not, I've got better things to do than hang around outside all afternoon."

"Were we actually having a chat?" Osian decided to lead the conversation, maybe keep the two almost brothers from going entirely off the rails. "You seemed more interested in poking at Chris. You mentioned something about Judge Allsop?"

"Don't think I said a name, did I?" Edgar smirked, then walked past them, jogging up the steps into his place and slamming the door behind him.

"Short chat." Osian stared at the closed door for a few seconds before turning to Dannel and Chris. "He did mention someone close to Judie Sharrow. So who else fits the bill other than Judge Allsop?"

"He's not the only person who meets the incredibly loose criteria." Chris had his phone out. His fingers tapped furiously against the screen. "I'm sending a message to a friend of mine in Florida. I want him to keep a closer eye on Tamsyn until I can visit."

"Abandoning us for sunnier lands?"

"If only temporarily." Chris spent another minute on his message before finishing up. "Let me give you a lift home. This is a dead end."

"Maybe." Osian waited until they'd gotten into

Chris's vehicle to grab his own phone. "I'm going to see if Abra can get any more information out of Judge Abbey. She'd know if Judie Sharrow was friendly with anyone other than Handsy Hamster."

And maybe she'll be open to giving us more dirt on Allsop.

What else do we have?

Nothing.

Aside from two family members who might go to jail if we can't figure it out. Is Wayne family? Stop poking holes in your own theories while you're talking to yourself.

TWENTY-FOUR

DANNEL

ABRA, IT TURNED OUT, DIDN'T HAVE ANY MORE information. She'd suggested they try to stop by the judge's office themselves. Dannel didn't like their chances.

"Rolly texted me." Dannel skimmed through the message while Chris navigated London traffic. "They've managed to clear up the footage of who dropped off Wayne's vehicle."

"And?"

"It's not Rolly or Wayne," Dannel stated what they'd all already known for a fact.

"Then who is it?" Osian twisted around in the front seat to glance back at him. "Can they see who the driver is?"

"Wayne believes it's one of the security guards—

not Edgar Smith, though." Dannel waited patiently for the rest of his brother's message. "Apparently, the police pulled CCTV from further down the road. The driver dropped someone off before continuing on."

"Any idea who the passenger was?" Chris asked before muttering curses when a black cab cut them off.

"Wayne thinks it's Edgar Smith. The video never shows the person's face. They walk in the direction of Wayne's flat, but CCTV never catches them again." Dannel frowned at his phone. "Why would he be dropped off a distance away then go to the flat anyway?"

"Maybe he didn't want to be seen re-entering the building? The footage we've already seen clearly shows him arriving with Willa, then leaving." Osian had his own phone out. "Is it possible he found a way inside without being seen?"

"Anything is possible." Chris punched his horn a few times when he was once again cut off in traffic. "Does no one know how to drive?"

"I wonder if the police will pick up Edgar to ask questions." Osian ignored Chris's muttering.

"They might." Dannel sent a follow-up message

to his brother, who responded immediately. "Rolly has no idea. They won't tell him anything."

"They've no reason to pick him up," Chris, ever the voice of reason, interjected into their debate. "Leave it with me. I've an idea."

It was early evening when they arrived back at their flat after striking out trying to meet up with the judge. Either of them. Chris dropped them off, promising to let them know if he found anything else out. Despite Osian's attempts to push him for details, Chris refused to give them anything other than that he planned to visit with old friends.

They found a familiar face waiting for them.

"Haider's here." Dannel nudged Osian with his elbow, drawing his attention away from Chris's vehicle driving off to the detective inspector. "Looks like Ian's got a captive audience."

"Not sure who I feel sorry for the most." Osian chuckled. "Probably Haider. Not sure his training has prepared him for our Ian."

They watched Ian waving his arms animatedly in the middle of a story. Dannel wondered what had brought Haider out to their flat again. *How many times can he tell us to stay out of his investigation?*

Is he here to pretend to arrest us as well?

"Let's save him." Osian looped his arm around Dannel and walked toward Ian and Haider.

"Who are we saving?" Dannel muttered.

"Darlings!" Ian flourished his scarf in their direction, ignoring how it smacked Haider across the face. "Things are always so delightfully intriguing when you're around."

"Are you making a nuisance of yourself?" Dannel felt Osian press his face against his back while tried to hide his laughter. "Careful. He might lock you up."

"It wouldn't be the first time a handsome man has placed silver bracelets around my wrists." Ian blithely disregarded Haider's sudden coughing fit and Osian's laughter. "Besides, you should be thanking me. I've regaled the detective inspector with your brilliance."

"Are we supposed to find this comforting? We're not, right?" Dannel grabbed Osian by the wrist and forced him to stop hiding. "A little help."

"What?" Osian breathed out a few times before he was able to reel in his laughter. "Sorry. Detective Inspector Khan. Were you waiting for us? Or hoping for a sugar daddy?"

"Ossie." Dannel shoved his giggling fiancé.

"Or sugar granddaddy? Is that a thing?"

"He's missed his evening snack. We'll be going upstairs now." Dannel caught Osian by the wrist to lead him into their building. "You're welcome to join us, Haider. Bye, Ian."

"Haider's going to kill us." Osian snickered.

"Pretty sure it's against the law," Haider offered from behind them. "How can I keep you out of trouble if I'm in prison for killing you?"

"Fair point. Want tea or coffee?" Osian unlocked the door and waited for both Dannel and Haider to enter before following himself. "Or beer? Pretty sure we have a few bottles."

"I'm going to... shower." Dannel dropped his backpack by the door and fled down the hall into the bedroom.

Falling onto the bed, Dannel stared up at their ceiling. He'd gotten wrapped up in the drama with Osian being almost run over and the argument with Edgar. And as a result, he'd missed the signs of an impending shutdown.

He wanted his headphones. The ones left in the living room in his backpack. It seemed far away.

Very far away.

Oceans and deserts away.

Am I being hyperbolic?

"Brought you snacks." Osian gently opened the

bedroom door. He placed Dannel's headphones on the bed along with a couple of crisp packets. "I'll figure out what Haider wants."

Acknowledging Osian with a thumbs up, Dannel reached out to grab his headphones. He shoved them on and quickly switched on the noise cancelling. *Blissful silence.* It swirled around him, effectively shutting out the little sounds filling their flat.

He selected one of the packets of crisps. *Walkers Prawn Cocktail.* Snacks and a nap? It wouldn't solve all his problems, but it couldn't hurt.

His mind refused to settle. Dannel pondered over the details they knew for certain of the night Barnaby Sharrow died. Not that there were many.

Why does it feel like we've missed something?

What've we missed?

Or maybe it's who have we missed?

TWENTY-FIVE
OSIAN

"Is he okay?" Haider stood in the middle of their living room when Osian returned from checking on Dannel. "Should I go? I wouldn't want to mess up a routine."

"He'll be fine. Headphones and crisps. Be right as rain in a few hours." Osian headed into the kitchen. "Beer? Cake?"

"Are those my only options? If so, I fear greatly for your health." Haider sat at their table, watching Osian root around in the fridge. "No to both."

"Of course we've got more than beer and cake. There are crisps." Osian grinned at the detective. "Only joking. So, how can we help? You didn't come here for the sole purpose of being hit on by our neighbour."

"Where were you this afternoon? After almost being run over?"

Osian stood up slowly and closed the fridge door. He narrowed his eyes suspiciously at Haider's relaxed posture. *Too comfortable. Too tranquil.* "We went on a little drive. Trying to soothe my nerves. You could say we went to London to see the queen."

"Go anywhere particular in the city? Or just for a drive? In mid-afternoon traffic... in London." Haider folded his arms across his chest, leaning back in the chair casually. "Were you and Dannel alone on this lovely tour of the city?"

"When did my kitchen turn into an interrogation room?"

"Friendly questions. We are mates, right?" Haider waved off the offer of a beer. "DI Powell picked up an interesting report of a disturbance outside of Edgar Smith's home. Did the queen look like an overly muscled security officer?"

"You came all the way over here to ask if we took our private security friend to commune with one of his kind?" Osian busied himself making a couple sandwiches with part of a leftover roast Adelle had dropped off for them. "If this were an American crime show, I'd plead the fifth. How about I settle for a nice 'no comment.'"

From the disgruntled sigh, Osian assumed Haider wasn't amused by his joke. He hadn't purposefully attempted to try the detective's patience. Maybe a little. Plausible deniability covered a great many sins, after all.

Haider was a good bloke. A decent copper. One dedicated to finding the truth. Osian simply didn't trust the system within which their detective inspector friend had to function.

Innocent people went to prison on far less evidence than what they had on Wayne. They hadn't officially taken him and Roland off the suspect list. Osian refused to relax until that happened.

"I'm not the enemy," Haider spoke into the tense silence. "My goal is to find the truth. We believe Wayne's innocent."

"I'll hold my sigh of relief until it's official." Osian wrapped up one of the finished sandwiches and placed it in the fridge for Dannel for later. "Want one?"

"Listen, Osian." Haider ignored his offer. "I need you to trust me for a little while longer."

"I'm guessing what you really mean is you want me to stay out of your investigation." Osian grabbed his plate and slid into the chair across from Haider.

"We received an anonymous tip about the

Sharrow inquiry." Haider watched Osian intently, clearly expecting a reaction of some sort. "Anything you'd like to share?"

"Sandwich?" Osian held up the untouched half.

After rubbing his temples for a few seconds, Haider decided to throw in the towel. He got up. His parting words were a stern warning about playing detective inspector in a homicide case.

Osian nodded dutifully while escorting him out of the flat and downstairs. He followed Haider out to his vehicle, waiting until he'd pulled away from the kerb to turn around. "He's definitely going to kill us."

"Oz?"

"Holy—" Osian jolted away from the hand that seemed to come out of nowhere to grab him firmly by the shoulder. He spun around to find Chris, holding his side with one hand, dried blood on his face and freshly formed bruises everywhere. "Did you run into a rampaging elephant?"

"In London?"

"There's a zoo. Stranger things have happened." Osian rapidly assessed the injuries he could see. "Let's get you inside before someone decides to call the emergency services for you."

The walk up to the flat took several minutes. Chris stopped halfway up to catch his breath, leaning heavily against the wall. Osian wondered if maybe he should've insisted on taking Chris to the nearest hospital.

"Don't look so worried. I've had worse. Nothing's broken, not even my nose." Chris started up the stairs again. "I didn't want DI Khan to see me, so I waited for him to drive off. He'd have questions."

"I have questions." Osian followed him inside the flat. He'd left the door open. "Sit on the couch. I'll grab our first aid kit. It's freshly stocked since the last convention."

One of the things their first responder coalition did was provide medical help at various cosplay events and conventions. Osian might never want to work as a paramedic again, but he still had all the skills he'd learnt on the job.

His initial assessment proved correct. No broken bones. No cuts requiring stitches. Osian cleaned the blood off Chris's face, then patched him up. He grabbed a couple of packets of frozen veggies from the fridge for him.

"Low-tech solution." Osian tossed them over to him. "Put one on your face and one on your ribs. You'll thank me later. I'll get you water and parac-etamol to dull the pain."

"I'll be fine. Not my first bruised ribs." Chris

adjusted the bag of peas on his face. "I'll just make sure to not breathe too deeply for a while. Surprised you haven't asked any questions."

"All in good time." Osian dug a few pills out of his kit before packing everything up. He stowed it on the coffee table for the moment. "Here. Hold these while I grab you some water."

"Mind making me a coffee?" Chris sank into the cushions with a pained grunt. "Think I'm going to need something stronger than water."

"Maybe have the water first? Have you eaten anything? I've got sandwiches made." Osian ignored Chris's muttering and went into the kitchen. "Are you going to tell me the other person looks worse?"

"He does."

"Shall I hazard a guess and say you ran into Edgar?" Osian filled a cup of water and grabbed the sandwich he'd made for Dannel. "Here."

"Edgar ran into my fist."

"Seems like you ran into his as well." Osian handed over the water, set the plate on the coffee table, and made sure Chris had the paracetamol. "A few times."

"He was waiting in the car park outside my building." Chris swallowed down the pills with a grimace. "Seemed to be under the mistaken belief

I've provided evidence to the police about his involvement in the murder."

"Haider did mention an anonymous source." Osian dropped into the armchair across from the sofa, propping his feet up on the coffee table. "I've a feeling he thought it came from either Dannel or me."

"It certainly wasn't me," Chris insisted. He stared down at the sandwich before finally grabbing half. "So, someone's provided evidence against Edgar. No wonder he took a swing at me."

"And it wasn't us." Osian pondered the possibilities for a few seconds. "Who? I can't imagine Wayne or Roland found something without telling us."

"Edgar wasn't the only person involved in the crime. There's no honour among thieves."

"Is there no honour among thieves? I mean, where did the phrase come from? There has to be some honour amongst thieves." Dannel wandered into the living room with his headphones dangling from one hand while the other rubbed his eyes. "What've I missed?"

"Haider thinks there's a conspiracy, and Edgar went toe-to-toe with Chris." Osian gestured to the plate on the table. "I made you a sandwich, but he's slobbered on it."

"First, I don't slobber." Chris threw the dripping bag of peas at Osian, then grimaced when it pulled on his ribs. "Second, I've a feeling we should reach out to DI Khan."

"Why?"

"What do you think Edgar's going to do when he realises his co-conspirator or conspirators have left him holding the metaphorical knife?" Chris waited a few seconds, then continued when they didn't have an answer. "He has cash. I've no doubt he's got at least one or two false identities. Par for the course in his line of business. He'll be out of the country before DI Khan can even think about bringing him in for questioning."

"All right, James Bond, how do we get ahead of your archnemesis?" Dannel made his way into the kitchen and grabbed a container of leftovers. He popped them into the microwave for a minute. "Haider's going to read us the riot act."

"Again," Osian agreed. He wondered if their detective inspector friend might do more than lecture them. "I'll send him a message. He can't yell via text."

"Yes, he can. All caps." Dannel watched the seconds on the microwave slowly tick down on the bowl of casserole Adelle had dropped off for them. "You okay, Chris?"

"Peas are helping." Chris took the fresh bag of frozen veggies that Osian brought to him from the freezer. "I'll be fine. Edgar's worse off."

"In all fairness, we only have your word..." Osian trailed off when Chris scowled at him. "Sorry. I'll try to take this more seriously."

The operative word being try.

I will try and fail.

This is all too absurd not to find funny.

"Are you going to check your phone?" Dannel interrupted his thoughts. He grabbed his bowl when the microwave finally dinged. "Keeps beeping. Very annoying. Please make it stop."

Osian grabbed his phone off the cushion where he'd tossed it. "Ah. Haider's on his way. He apparently stopped down the street to grab something to eat."

"Brilliant. We've enough time to come up with a valid excuse for my mildly battered appearance."

"Mildly?" Dannel glanced over at him. He pointed his spoon at Chris. "This is mild?"

By the time Dannel finished eating his leftovers, Haider had arrived. Osian hesitated before opening the door. He had no idea what the reaction to Chris's bruises would be.

"Unbelievable," Haider muttered the second he stepped inside. He began grumbling to himself after getting a good look at Chris's bruised face. "You two are going to be the absolute death of me or my career."

It was slightly unfair. Osian didn't think they'd been personally involved in the fight. Chris had managed it all on his own.

If anything, they'd helped to clean up the mess. Or Osian had. Dannel had slept through the bandaging-up process.

"Oi. Hang on. James Bond, here, did this to himself. Well, not literally, but Dannel and I had zero involvement in the process of him getting his arse kicked." Osian glanced over at Chris when he coughed loudly. "Pardon me, in him kicking arse."

"Children, please." Haider put an immediate halt to Osian and Chris's playful banter. "Can you not?"

"He showed up like this." Osian gestured to Chris. "I invited him up out of the goodness of my heart. Look at him. He's injured."

"And I was asleep the entire time." Dannel held his hands up when Haider's glower swung in his direction. "Well, obviously not now. I woke up. We didn't punch him."

"So, who did and why?"

Deciding they all needed to take a breath, Osian went into the kitchen to put the kettle on. He grabbed a cake Dannel's auntie had brought over as well. A hot brew and a little sugar might sweeten Haider's mood.

Hopefully.

While Chris repeated an abbreviated version of his story for Haider, Osian poured everyone a mug of tea and set the cake on the coffee table. He sat on the couch with the largest slice for himself; he'd earned it.

"So, did you call in the anonymous tip?" Haider asked when Chris wrapped up his tale.

"Not I." Chris shook his head. "I've no concrete proof of his involvement, or I would've called you. And I'd have no need to be anonymous."

"And you two?" Haider sounded dubious. He narrowed his gaze when Dannel and Osian both shook their heads. "You sure?"

"I'm fairly confident I'd know if I called you." Osian still didn't know what the supposed tip had been about. "Maybe if you tell us what they said, we can help you figure out who it was."

"Nice try." Haider continued to scowl at them over the rim of his mug. "All I will tell you is we've enough evidence at this point to bring Edgar Smith in for questioning."

"Actual questioning or hypothetically pretend questions?" Dannel asked.

"Actual questioning." Haider set the mug down on the coffee table and grabbed the packet of food he'd brought with him, starting to eat his dinner. "We plan to send uniformed officers around to his place in the morning. Not a word from any of you, though. I won't have you buggering up my case."

"Okay, rude. We'd never purposefully muck things up for you." Osian had to hide his grin behind his mug. He took a sip of tea. "Edgar Smith isn't really a fan of any of us. He's not likely to reach out to us."

"Keep it that way." Haider managed to seem completely serious while pointing a drooping chip in his direction. "I've almost gotten Wayne officially removed from the suspect list and shifted into a witness. Let me do my job."

TWENTY-SIX

DANNEL

"Haider's back."

Dannel sat up in bed slowly, blinking at the blurry figure by the bedroom door. "What? It's not even light out. We haven't had coffee. When did the doorbell ring? What is happening?"

"Okay, take a breath. You're rambling. I don't think Haider cares about it being six in the sodding morning." Osian grabbed a T-shirt from the floor and tossed it to Dannel. "He wants a chat with both of us."

"In pyjamas?" Dannel dragged the shirt over his head. He was definitely going to need coffee to cope with an early morning interrogation. "Why?"

"Not sure he cares one way or another as long as

we aren't starkers." Osian headed for the door. "I've got coffee just about made."

Flopping back on the bed, Dannel stared up at the ceiling for a few seconds. *What could've possibly happened overnight to drag Haider here again? Did Chris get in another brawl with his murderous almost half-sibling? I'll never know if I don't get out of bed.*

His curiosity and anxiety won out, forcing him to roll out of bed. Dannel paused to pull up the sheet and blanket. He stumbled down the hall to find Haider pacing in the living room.

Well, yes, he does seem agitated.

More so than usual.

"Coffee." Osian shoved a mug into Dannel's hand and offered a second to Haider. "Why exactly are you here before the sun comes up? We've retired. No one needs us up this early, aside from our mums. I mean, we haven't even had time to bugger up your case yet."

"Edgar Smith vanished into thin air." Haider dropped the bombshell, then watched them over the rim of his mug. "Anything you'd like to share with me?"

"Oh...." Dannel dropped heavily onto the sofa. He barely managed to avoid coffee sloshing everywhere. "Is he a wizard?"

"Dannel." Osian pressed his lips together in a blatant attempt not to grin. "How did he vanish? Was it an abracadabra sort of situation or more using fake passports to slip out of the country?"

"Wizard," Dannel muttered with a snicker.

"Are you both quite finished?" Haider sounded one step away from having a good shout at them. Dannel wondered if it might help the detective inspector relieve some stress. "Did you see or hear anything last night?"

"Could you be more specific? I saw Ossie's bollocks, but I'm not sure that's what you mean." Dannel glanced at the stunned detective inspector. "Right. Definitely not what you meant."

Osian had to stop cackling like a hyena to answer. "Chris left not long after you did last night. He'd suffered enough for one day. We were home the rest of the evening. Edgar wouldn't have confided in any of us. Threatened, maybe, but not likely to share his plans to make a break for it. How'd you know he fled?"

"We believe he boarded a private jet sometime early this morning." Haider's gaze stayed on Dannel, who lifted his mug to hide from him.

"We don't have one of those. Also, Edgar Smith's a murderous wanker, so we wouldn't have helped him if we did." Osian drew Haider's attention away from Dannel. He relaxed into the sofa with a sigh of relief. "None of us would've aided and abetted a killer."

"Maybe not intentionally."

"Okay." Dannel reached forward to set the mug on the coffee table. He hadn't woken up enough yet to decide if Haider seriously believed they'd help Edgar. "How do you unintentionally help a killer? He ran Ossie over. I'd help him into the Thames before I'd help him hop on a plane. Sodding detectives with sodding theories."

"Dannel." Osian came over to place a hand on his shoulder. "Haider's our friend. Not sure he appreciates us telling him to sod off with his carefully thought out theories."

"Our house. Six in the sodding morning. I'll sod what I want," Dannel grumped. "Sounded better in my head."

"How do you sod what you want?" Osian grinned down at him.

"Could you two focus for five seconds?" Haider interrupted before Dannel could respond.

"Not without coffee. Have you told Chris yet?" Dannel couldn't help wondering if Edgar had headed for Florida. He had threatened to pay their half-sister a visit. "He'll want to know."

"Tamsyn." Osian sent a worried glance at Dannel. He'd clearly had the same thought. He disappeared down the hall and returned a moment later with his phone. "I'll text him."

Picking up his coffee, Dannel went into the kitchen, since they definitely needed something other than caffeine. It might improve his mood. Early mornings weren't his favourite thing.

Scrounging around in the fridge, Dannel realized they'd put off a grocery shop for too long. The cupboards were bare. Breakfast would either be left-overs or delivery at this point.

"Oi. Ossie. Tell Chris to meet us here. I'm starved. We can have something delivered." Dannel had no doubt Osian had already convinced Chris to meet up with them. He glanced over at Haider, who'd been whispering to Osian. "Are you staying?"

"I've a case to solve."

"Is that a yes or a no? I mean, you did bang on our door at six in the morning. So clearly, you think the case will be solved with our help." Dannel took the phone when Osian tossed it over to him. "Any special requests?"

"Get doubles of everything we'd usually order.

Maybe triples if you're starved." Osian nodded. He peered over at Haider. "And yes, I have shared your bit of news with Chris. You're too late to surprise him with the news about Eddie the Eagle. I didn't give him any specifics, though. Just said there was a development with Edgar."

"You're not even half as funny as you think you are." Haider's smile seemed to state otherwise. "Fine. I'm staying. I've got to ask Chris questions anyway."

Breakfast arrived five minutes after Chris. Dannel was on his second mug of coffee. They made an uncomfortably awkward quartet around the table.

"Lovely weather we're having." Dannel tried to smile, though he had a feeling it was more of a grimace from the snicker Osian let out. "What? It is nice for London in November."

"What's going on?" Chris definitely didn't want to play at small talk with them. Dannel, for one, was relieved. "Did something happen to Wayne?"

"Have you seen Edgar Smith in the last ten hours or so?" Haider had a gift for making important questions seem innocuous.

For his part, Dannel wouldn't have hesitated to answer. Chris did. He set his fork down and leaned forward with his elbows resting on the table.

Chris pointed a finger at the bruise on his face. "I

haven't seen him since he showed up at my place. We're not friends, Inspector."

"He fled the country on a plane," Dannel offered, earning a glower from Haider and a chuckle from Osian. "What? You were getting there eventually, right? The anticipation is driving me up the wall."

"Edgar? Fled the country? When?" Chris sat up and immediately reached for his phone resting on the table. Haider stretched an arm across the table to grab it from him. "What the—"

"Do not go all John Wick on us at the kitchen table." Osian placed a hand on Chris's arm when he went to stand up. "Easy there. We're all friends."

"Thought I was James Bond?"

"Not with the look I saw on your face when he snatched your mobile." Osian gently but firmly eased Chris down into his chair. "Edgar's not going to answer your call."

"I wasn't going to call the arrogant wanker." Chris knocked his knuckles against the table and held his hand out. "I'm more concerned about where the hell he's gone. Do you know any details about his flight?"

"Private jet." Dannel continued to ignore the

exasperated glare being sent in his direction from Haider. "They think."

"His family doesn't have one themselves." Chris continued to hold his hand out until Haider returned his phone. "They've friends who do. It wouldn't take much to convince them to give him a ride anywhere around the world if his father asked. His less than savoury connections would do it for a price as well."

"Who are you texting?" Osian asked while Chris continued tapping out a rapid-fire message on his phone. His fingers hit hard enough that Dannel wondered if he was going to damage the screen. "Tamsyn?"

"She hates phone calls and early mornings and late nights and just about everything if I'm honest. If I text her, she'll be less likely to rip my head off when I see her." Chris set his phone on the table. He kept periodically checking for a response. "If he's fled the country, you might want to contact your American counterparts. He threatened to pay her a visit."

Haider pulled his notebook out of his pocket along with a pen. "Can you tell me where your sister lives? Then I can reach out to local detectives. They'll be able to make sure she's safe and see if Edgar's approached her."

"What exactly was this anonymous tip?" Chris

asked. Dannel held his breath, figuring Haider would be more likely to give a detailed answer.

"Missing CCTV footage from a shop across from where the murder occurred." Haider tossed his notebook to Chris for him to write down Tamsyn's details. He held his phone out to show them a still image. "Here's the alley itself. The video shows enough for me to have a warrant for Edgar Smith's arrest."

Convenient.

How convenient for someone to show up with evidence now when the police have moved on from Wayne.

Throwing Edgar under the bus as a distraction.

"I'll need to speak with your sister." Haider broke into Dannel's thoughts.

"Not a chance in hell." Chris shook his head immediately.

There was a silent conversation happening between the two men. Dannel didn't understand it. He watched the way Haider and Chris glowered at each other for several uncomfortably long minutes.

"Pretty sure this is the point in a romcom when they kiss." Osian grinned mischievously at Dannel. They both broke out laughing when Chris shoved him out of his seat. "Oi. Committing assault in front of a copper? Brave."

"He's not harassing my sister. And he's definitely got more to share about the Sharrow case." Chris flung the notebook back to Haider. "The city she lives in. I'm not giving you her number."

"What I have is a case to solve, and I've already shared more than I should." Haider pocketed his notebook and got to his feet. "I might need to speak with your sister."

"You might need to leave her the hell alone."

Dannel exchanged a worried glance with Osian. They didn't need the conversation escalating into something more. "We're on the same side."

"Not if he's planning to bother my little sister," Chris grumbled protectively.

"An unnamed high court judge has been brought in for questioning today. Sources close to the investigation tell us the person may be involved in the murder of barrister Barnaby Sharrow. The detectives have apparently been following a trail of corruption to the accused. More details to follow as they become available to us."

"An unnamed high court judge?" Dannel grabbed the remote and switched off the telly. "Haider's moved quickly on this. I wonder if they managed to catch up with Edgar."

"Not according to Chris." Osian checked their group chat to find it buzzing with comments from everyone who'd seen the news report. Wayne had suggested meeting up to discuss things in person, making him wonder what their solicitor friend had heard. "Edgar hasn't shown up in Florida, which is all he cares about."

"So how have they managed to bring the judge in for questioning?"

Osian finished typing a response to Wayne's comment in the group chat. "Fancy going out for lunch?"

"We literally just ate lunch."

"Second lunch?" Osian leaned over the back of the sofa to brush his lips against Dannel's neck. "Have you seen the group chat?"

"Nope." Dannel read through the messages when Osian held his phone out for him. "I suppose we could eat again. Cake. There's always room for dessert."

"Second lunch it is."

After confirming a time and place with the group, Osian convinced Dannel to join him for a quick bath. His favourite way to get clean. They made it out of their flat already a few minutes late and ran into Ian on the stairs.

"Morning. Or afternoon. I've lost track of time."

"Hello, darlings. Have you heard the news about the handsy judge?"

"We did." Dannel finished locking up the flat and joined Osian.

"I find it odd Allsop capitulated so readily when I confronted him." Ian meticulously fixed his cravat, then continued down the stairs. "So easy, not even a fight. If one were guilty of murder, one would put up more of a fight. And now he's been arrested."

"One would," Osian said with a teasing grin.

"Impudent wretch. What I am attempting to say is perhaps you might want to look at those around the judge." Ian smiled his thanks when Osian held the door open for him. Dannel followed them outside. "I'm not sure the police have the right man, after all."

"I'm sure they'll get the whole story." Osian found it hard to believe the judge hadn't been involved, based on everything they knew about him.

"I'm off to rehearsals. Toodles, darlings." Ian sauntered off, waving his scarf at them over his shoulder.

They watched him leave. Ian always knew how to make a grand entrance and exit. Osian grabbed his phone when the jaunty tune he'd selected for Abra went off.

"Apparently, they want to meet a little later. We've got at least an hour. Want to swing by the alley Haider mentioned? Check out the potential crime scene?" Osian looped his finger around one of Dannel's backpack straps, falling in step with him. "Maybe the police missed something?"

"Not sure Haider will appreciate your lack of faith in his investigative abilities." Dannel paused by the window of the Ortea family shop to wave at his auntie. "We could walk. It's not all that far. We can always grab an Uber to the pub when we're done."

"I'm more concerned about Haider not appreciating our playing detective." Osian knew their detective inspector friend worried about them. "We should become licensed private investigators."

"Do they need licenses?"

"Must do." Osian shrugged. "We should look into it. He can't complain about our investigating then."

"Want to bet?" Dannel did have a point with his scepticism.

"Not really, no."

From the little information they'd garnered out of Haider, the police obviously believed Barnaby Sharrow had been murdered in an alley not far from the pub. But had he been led there? Forced? Or had Edgar followed him and struck at an opportune time?

They found the alley. Osian had recognised it from the image Haider showed them. Not hard to find.

Setting his backpack on the ground, Dannel grabbed their camera. He began filming the alley. A good idea; they could use the footage for an upcoming podcast episode.

With Dannel busy, Osian began pacing the alley. *No, we don't look suspicious at all. Please, people of London, don't call the police on us. We're not criminals.*

Laughing to himself, Osian checked out the brick walls on either side. He had no idea what he expected to find. Mostly, he was trying to visualise what had happened the night of the murder.

"How'd I know you'd be here?" Chris drew Osian out of his inspection of the brick wall. "DI Khan know you're mucking about in his crime scene?"

"There are no mucks to be had. Also, no caution tape. Or police." Dannel paused in his filming of the alley. "We're going to do a podcast episode on Barnaby's death."

They'd done a post-mortem breakdown of the theatre caper. They'd detailed the mayhem at the

Evelyn Lavelle. Ian had even been on with them. He'd been a hit with their subscribers.

On their website, they'd begun to include more details about the cases. Podcasts tended to run too long if they spoke about everything they'd uncovered in their research. Dannel's video would make an excellent addition to the Barnaby Sharrow episode.

A bit macabre, maybe, but it was a true-crime podcast. People didn't come to them for sunshine and tulips. Murder was a grim business.

"How'd you find us?" Dannel went back to filming without waiting to listen.

"Abra." Chris scowled when Osian snickered at him. "Don't. We're just friends."

"Oh, very friendly." Osian winked at him. He laughed again when Chris rolled his eyes. "Did you get a hold of your sister?"

"She finally texted me earlier. She's off on a fishing trip, apparently, and promised to let me know when they're back on dry land." Chris didn't seem overly comforted by his sister's response. "I can't shake the feeling Edgar's headed her way."

"Why?" Osian moved toward the end of the alley where Chris stood. "Did she say something else? Did he?"

"No, nothing like that. It's just, Tamsyn has an

impressive trust fund. Combined inheritances from several wealthy relatives. If he's desperate and cut off from his bank account..."

"She's an easy target." Dannel joined them. He pressed the backpack into Osian's hands so he could put the camera away.

"Easier than just about any other option." Chris nodded. "And he knows how much she has access to."

"Hello there. Mr Garey?" a scruffy-looking young man called out to them when they stepped fully out of the alley. He shuffled over, fidgeting with the frayed edges of his jacket. "You might not remember me."

"Mattie? Right?" Osian remembered the early-morning emergency call a year and a half ago. They'd gone to a park near one of the more dodgy nightclubs. "Someone smashed a bottle on your head."

Mattie had been sleeping on a bench. Drunken fools had lobbed a bottle and caught him on the back of the head. Osian had helped him find a better place to stay after getting him to the hospital.

"Got a job now. And a flat. Well, a room, but it's mine. Doing all right for myself. I listen to your podcast while I'm working nights." Mattie grinned proudly. He nodded his head toward the alley. "Saw fancy coppers earlier. They told me to jog on and didn't give me a chance to tell my story."

"We're all ears." Dannel spoke for the three of them. "Not literally, of course. We have other body parts."

"Dannel." Osian placed a hand on his arm, tugging him back against his chest. "Go on, Mattie. What'd you see?"

Leaning in close, Mattie explained he'd been walking home after his shift at work. A commotion across the street had caught his attention. He'd noticed two men helping a third into the back seat of a vehicle; the latter had been passed out drunk.

Or so Mattie had assumed.

In the dark, would a dead body have hung as limply as a drunken one?

"I couldn't see their faces. But I did spot a second car on the same side as the street as me. Fancy sports car. Some kind of Mercedes, I think. Not good with makes or models. A man was in the driver seat, with a woman in the back being chauffeured around." Mattie shoved his hands into his pockets, shifting from one foot to the other. "They took off once the others left. Opposite directions, though. It seemed odd. We don't usually see two luxury vehicles around here, especially not so early in the morning."

Two vehicles? And a mystery woman?

Is the mistress or the spurned wife involved?

Is Ian right, after all?

After saying goodbye to Mattie, who promised to "speak with the fancy coppers" about what he saw, they decided to head to the pub. Chris drove. Cheaper and more convenient than an Uber. Osian wasn't about to complain.

"I had a chance to chat with my mate, Robert, again. Their office is buzzing about Edgar's disappearance. No one wants to admit to knowing anything, apparently." Chris made sure they'd both buckled up before easing out of his parking space. "Rumour is he left under the guise of playing private security to some billionaire. No one would've looked twice at him boarding a plane."

"Bugger." Osian wondered if the police had any chance of finding Edgar. "He could be anywhere at this point."

TWENTY-EIGHT

DANNEL

"Cheers." Abra raised her glass to their crowded table at the pub. They'd actually had to drag two together to fit everyone. "We've got nothing but beers and terrible plans."

"What was wrong with my plan?" Osian had sunk into his chair with his head resting against Dannel's shoulder. "Sure, it lacked a few of the finer details. But it's better than what anyone else had."

"Try all of the details. All you've got is a code name for your plan." Dannel held his beer out of reach when Osian went for it. "We have three things to do. First, see if Willa knows anything else. Second, follow up with Abra's godmum. And last, try to see if Chris's contacts know anything about the mystery woman being chauffeured around the scene of the crime. It can't be a coincidence."

They needed answers.

More answers.

Mattie's account of the night had brought up so many more questions. It also gave some credence to Ian's doubts about Judge Allsop's involvement. Dannel believed he might still be connected to the crime, but maybe he wasn't the only one.

"Divide and conquer, then," Osian interjected into the conversation bouncing around between their gathered group of friends. "Abra can go with Chris to have a chat with her godmum, then speak to his spy friends. We can go with Wayne to speak with Willa."

"You've got to meet up with your mum and Olivia. Wedding plans?" Dannel reminded him. They'd played six rounds of rock, paper, scissors before Osian finally lost.

"Bugger." Osian chugged down the last of his beer, then reached over to steal Dannel's. "Don't whinge. I'm going to need the fortification. Also, we need a better decision-making system than rock, paper, scissors."

"You only complain when you lose." Dannel laughed when Osian flicked a bottle cap at him. "No more beers. We can't solve crimes if we're sloshed."

"Pretty sure a fair number of detectives would disagree with you." Roland held his hands up in surrender when they both scowled at him. "Are we all leaving together?"

With an exaggerated sigh and kiss to Dannel's head, Osian disappeared from the pub to his dreaded meeting. Dannel and Roland stayed together when Wayne got a message from the office. They'd left Abra and Chris alone.

Accidentally on purpose playing at matchmaking.

Though, Dannel wasn't sure it would prove successful. Chris hadn't been himself entirely. He'd checked his phone every few seconds, obviously worried about his sister.

There was every chance Chris would leave for Florida. He wouldn't be able to relax until Edgar was safely behind bars. Dannel couldn't blame him, not after Osian's close call and Barnaby Sharrow's death.

"Stop worrying about Osian. I'm sure an afternoon of wedding planning torture won't damage him too badly." Roland threw an arm around Dannel's shoulders. "Pretty sure your Oz can handle his mum and sister. Though, you could always keep eloping as a backup plan."

"And be murdered by our mums? No, thanks."

Dannel shoved his brother away. "Have you heard anything about your suspension?"

"Nothing." Roland sighed heavily. "What if they never let me back, Danny? My whole damn career over for nothing at all."

"Rolly."

"You had ideas for what to do when you retired. I've got nothing." Roland rubbed the back of his neck. "Wayne says I shouldn't stress about things that haven't happened."

"He's not wrong." Dannel was being slightly hypocritical, given how much he worried about stuff all the time. "We are a family of worriers."

"True enough."

They'd driven halfway to Wayne's flat when the man in question sent another text. Willa had shown up at his office. Roland quickly found a street to turn down, allowing them to change directions.

When they arrived, they found Willa and Wayne making awkward small talk. It seemed to involve them sitting across from each other in her office and pretending neither existed. Dannel could relate.

He spent a lot of time pretending not to be involved in a conversation unless absolutely required to speak. Thankfully, Osian was usually there to rescue him. Despite being a gifted solicitor, Wayne didn't appear to be interested in using his usual eloquence.

"Tell us about the night at the pub." Dannel didn't want to waste an entire afternoon trying to dance around the subject. "Anything you might've forgotten or didn't think was important?"

"Still playing detectives, are we? Fine. I shall play along with this charade if I must." Willa rolled her eyes in a way that reminded Dannel of a teenage Olivia when she'd been tired of her brother's nonsense. "I do remember Eddie chatting up one of the wives. Not sure which one, though. I didn't see her face."

"One of the wives?" Roland asked.

"Eddie's security detail occasionally included the spouses of judges and barristers. Usually during high-profile cases or when threats were made." Willa began flipping through a stack of files on her desk. "The wives definitely enjoyed his presence."

"Anyone in particular?" Wayne leaned forward, suddenly far more interested in the conversation.

"All of them? He's handsome. Comes from a connected family. And fit. Have you seen his body? Pretty confident the wives weren't the only ones interested." Willa plucked a folder from the middle of the pile. "Are we finished? I have a client consultation in a mo, and I'd like to be prepared for it. So go play police in your own office."

One of the wives?

Which one?

Sharrow's? The judge's? Someone we haven't even thought of?

Judie Sharrow had a motive to get rid of her husband. Judge Allsop's wife, Clarissa, might want to frame her husband, but why kill Barnaby?

Had Wayne been collateral damage? A convenient person to blame the crime on? Or, since they knew Edgar had been involved at least in disposing of the body, had he been the one to want to frame Wayne?

Maybe the killer had decided to improvise.

Was throwing Edgar to the wolves a last-ditch effort to escape being discovered?

Every step of the way seemed to involve more questions than answered. Dannel didn't think they'd ever get to the bottom of the mystery. But then again, money and power always tended to make things more complicated.

"Let's head to my office." Wayne motioned for them to follow him. "We can chat in private."

Guiding them through the labyrinth of desks,

offices, and hallways, Wayne showed them to his office, followed them in, and closed the door. Dannel sank into one of the plush leather seats. He briefly wondered if wedding planning would've been the more straightforward task.

Deal with our mums and Olivia, who all have hearts in their eyes?

Or a murderer?

On the whole, I'd almost rather deal with a murderer.

Roland held a hand up to stop Wayne, who'd been grumbling about Willa. He scanned a message on his phone. "Chris had an accident?"

"Are you asking or telling us?" Dannel leaned over to try to read the message for himself.

"Abra's making it sound more like an incident than an accident." Roland held out the phone so Dannel could see. "They're already at the hospital."

"We should go." Dannel got to his feet quickly. "Text Ossie. He'll want to know."

"He'll want to get out of wedding planning, you mean." Roland grinned.

"WILL YOU QUIT GRINNING? WE'RE RUSHING TO see one of our friends who was hurt." Olivia swatted him on the arm. "It's obscene."

"What? I owe him a beer. He got me away from wedding planning insanity. What happened to keeping things simple?" Osian caught his sister when she stumbled over an uneven patch of pavement. "We asked for your help because we wanted less madness. Not more."

"Have you tried getting our mum and Dannel's to listen? When they're together thinking about the wedded bliss of their beloved firstborn sons?" She poked him in the side. "Not one word of complaint. You threw me to the wolves."

"What happened to 'I'm Princess Olivia, and I rule the world'?"

"Princess Olivia was slain by the dragons."

"I'm telling Mum you called her a dragon." Osian danced away from his sister when she went to punch him. "Now who's being obscene on the way to the hospital?"

"Can you pretend you're thirty and not three? For once?" She caught up to him and looped her arm around his. "I have an idea about the wedding."

"Okay?"

"You two sneak off to get married at the register office. Mums and immediate family attending. Then we'll book some venue and throw a massive party." Olivia sounded far too confident.

"You've already booked a place, haven't you?"

"Just make plans for a spectacular cosplay wedding reception, all right?" She patted his arm with the air of someone who controlled the universe. "I'll manage everything, even the dragon mums."

"Is it sneaking off to get married if everyone knows the plan?"

"Don't rain on my dramatic parade, Osian Garey." She winked when he grumbled under his breath at her. "Hey, see, he's obviously okay if he's outside the hospital."

Following her gaze, Osian noticed a bandaged-up Chris in an argument with Abra. He didn't need to hear the conversation to know what was happening. Abra was in full paramedic mode dealing with a difficult patient.

"I am fine." Chris spoke each word with increasing irritation. "I didn't require stitches or a scan of any sort."

"They hit you over the head with a brick."

"Glancing blow." Chris waved off the concern. He nodded at Osian and Olivia when they stepped closer. "Hello, you two."

"How do you receive a glancing blow from a brick?" Abra glowered at him.

"Abs makes a most excellent point." Osian decided to intervene before the conversation went from entertaining to heated. "Who grazed your noggin?"

"Not a clue." Chris began to walk away. "Come on. We've parked down the street. Wayne sent a text inviting us to his place. Roland and Dannel are meeting us there. We'll tell you about our adventure on the way there."

On the drive over, Chris gave an abbreviated version of what happened. Abra immediately interjected with a fuller picture. Osian tried not to laugh at their bickering with each other.

Like an old married couple.

The two had struck out with Abra's godmum. She'd had nothing to share. Chris had then suggested they stop by Edgar's place of employment. They'd been on their way back to his vehicle when someone quite literally chucked a brick at him, catching Chris on the side of the head and his shoulder.

"You're bloody lucky they didn't have better aim." Abra still sounded put out.

"'Bloody' being the operative word?" Osian could see dried blood along Chris's hairline and on his shirt. He reached up to put a comforting hand on Abra's shoulder. "Easy there, Abs. I'm sure our James Bond can dodge bullets, so he'll be just fine."

"Well, he couldn't dodge a brick."

"Ouch. Brutal." Osian grinned. "Are you saying he's—"

"Whatever terrible joke you're about to share, maybe don't?" Abra pinched his hand, causing him to yank it back. "I can hear it now. Something about being one brick short of a load?"

"Okay, rude. Also, spooky mind-reading skills are cheating." Osian rubbed his hand. "Aren't we supposed to avoid causing pain in others? Paramedics and all that? Dedicated to healing?"

"Did you find anything out before someone bashed in your skull?" Olivia interjected. She sent a warning glare in Osian's direction. "Anyone at Edgar's willing to chat?"

"Without the side of brick?" Osian couldn't help adding.

No one had been willing to talk. Chris claimed even his friends at the private security firm had clammed up. They'd closed ranks around Edgar.

Maybe they weren't aiding in his escape, but they also had no interest in sharing information.

"Wayne wants to know if we're in a pizza or Nando's sort of mood. They're going to stop by to pick up whatever we decide on." Abra held up her phone. "I'm voting for pizza."

"Same," Osian agreed. He kept thinking about what Mattie had said.

I can't let this go. Mattie saw a woman being chauffeured around. If Edgar did kill Barnaby and handled disposing of the body, who was driving her vehicle? It had to have been someone he trusted not to tell the police.

Who can help us figure out which woman was involved?

Digging through his backpack for his phone, Osian decided to message Ian. He might be able to find a way to meet up with Judie Sharrow and Clarissa Allsop. People of their sort were always going out for drinks.

Ian: Oh, Darling, Are we going on an adventure again? I've just the scarf for a night of intrigue.

Osian: How soon can you set something up?

Ian: Would this evening be too soon? I've theatre business to discuss with the lady Allsop. She's quite a patron of the arts. I'll see if she's willing to meet up with us somewhere.

Patron of the arts?

Yes, but has she been a patron of murder as well?

"Can you drop me off at home first? I've got to chat with Ian about something." Osian tapped Chris on the shoulder, who nodded. "I'll meet everyone at Wayne's after."

The drive through Covent Garden took long

enough that Osian considered simply getting out and walking. Traffic in London was always such a beast. He eventually got out and waved off his friends.

He sent a text to Dannel, explaining why he'd be late. Chris (and probably Abra as well) would've attempted to change his mind. Dannel understood his desire to want answers immediately.

An hour later, Ian and Osian were in a Rolls-Royce being driven across London to meet with Judie Sharrow and Clarissa Allsop. He managed to catch a sneaky photo of the chauffer to message to both Mattie and Chris. The former, unfortunately, couldn't say for sure if he was the driver he'd seen the night of the murder.

No matter how hard Osian tried, he couldn't quite shake the sense of trepidation. One of the women had definitely been involved in the murder. They had to be; nothing else made sense at all.

"Here we are, darling." Ian tapped Osian on the arm. They'd pulled up outside the Allsop home not far from Regent's Park. "How long do you think this has been in the Allsop family?"

"Long before either of us were born, my dear." Ian led him up the steps toward the front door, which a butler had already opened. "Theirs is a whole other world."

Clarissa Allsop was the epitome of grace and refinement. She welcomed them into a luxurious drawing room, offering tea or wine. Ian accepted the latter; Osian politely declined. "Now, how can I be of assistance?"

Settled onto the most uncomfortable sofa in history, Osian tried to find a subtle way to weasel answers out of her. He glanced over at Ian, who immediately nattered on about an upcoming theatre charity event. *Bless him. He is adept at the conversation game, isn't he?*

The two chatted cordially like old friends who had secrets to hide. Osian found his opening into the conversation when she mentioned her husband's absence. *Busy? Busy with the small matter of a police interrogation because you set him up for murder?*

"Did you know Edgar Smith well?" Osian kept his tone innocently curious.

She turned pale blue eyes in his direction. Her mouth tightened slightly before lifting into the ghost of a smile. "The security chap? He drove my Rolls several times before Hamnet poached him and my vehicle for his own use. So I've another driver now."

Do you?

Were you out with him the night of the murder?

"What do you drive now?"

"Me? Drive?" Clarissa scoffed. She took a delicate sip of wine. "My vehicle is a lovely Mercedes of some sort. I've never bothered with names."

A Mercedes?

Really?

"Were you close with the Sharrows?" Osian decided they'd tiptoed around the tulips for long enough. They needed a more direct question. "Barnaby and Judie?"

Clarissa carefully set her glass on the little round table beside her chair. "I'm acquainted with them. Everyone knows everyone. Don't they?"

"They do." Ian smiled while subtly nudging Osian's shoe with his own.

"Will you excuse me for a moment?" She got to her feet and exited through a side door that Osian hadn't noticed earlier when the butler had directed them into the room.

With a second to themselves, Osian took a moment to snoop around the elegantly decorated drawing room. It looked like something off the set of a period drama. Something out of a magazine. Not a home but a museum dedicated to a different time.

How do people live like this? Vapid, empty mansions with nothing surrounding them but uncomfortable wealth.

"What do you think, darling? Is she the one?"

Osian stopped his perusal of a painting on the wall to glance at Ian, who remained sitting on the couch. *Is it a couch? Do toffs have a fancier name for it? Probably.* "I've no idea."

Part of him wanted to say yes. Clarissa Allsop had definitely reacted when he'd mentioned Edgar and Judie. Just a slight twitch of her lips. A tightening around her eyes. Nothing massive but enough for him to want to know why.

Continuing his snooping, Osian moved to the bookshelf across from the painting. He found a series of photos in gilded frames. None had the happy couple together. One, in particular, drew his attention.

Why would there be a photo of Clarissa being escorted into an event by Edgar Smith? Shouldn't it be her husband? Intriguing. What exactly was going on with these people?

"Osian, darling?" Ian's voice was suddenly filled with tension.

It reminded him of the night down the well.

Osian turned away from the painting and found Clarissa pointing a double-barrelled hunting rifle at them. "You planned the murder with Edgar Smith."

"Clever boy. We've watched you. Tried to warn you off." She shook her head at him.

Osian shifted away from the bookcase to get closer to Ian, who sat frozen on the sofa. "Why turn Edgar in if you'd planned it together? And why frame Wayne?"

"The solicitor wasn't supposed to even be involved. Edgar had disliked him; something about an argument about how he handled security at the office once, but I told him to blame Hamnet and his strumpet. Then the little fool went and fell in love with her," Clarissa spat the words out as if they hurt her. "I refused to allow him to get away with it."

Little fool.

Edgar?

Tall bloke built like a rugby player?

Maybe I should be paying closer attention to the homicidal toff in front of me.

"Edgar fell in love with Judie Sharrow." Osian wanted to keep her talking. She might be less likely to shoot them with her antique rifle, probably a family heirloom left over from hunting days gone by. "He double-crossed you."

"In a manner of speaking. I couldn't allow them to escape unpunished." She shifted the weapon in her arm slightly. "Imagine the humiliation."

I'm imagining something.

How have I dragged Ian into yet another life-threatening situation? We barely survived the last one.

"And now I have to deal with you both. Pity."

THIRTY

"Is everything all right?" Chris stepped over to Dannel, who'd sequestered himself in the corner of Wayne's flat away from everyone. "You seem tense."

"I'm always tense in social situations."

"Tenser than normal," he countered.

Dannel rubbed the back of his neck uneasily. He hadn't heard from Osian in over an hour despite having messaged him a few times. "Ossie's not responding to my texts."

"Wasn't he just swinging by your flat to pick something up?" Chris narrowed his eyes suspiciously at his shrug. "Dannel? Where did he go?"

"To visit Ian?"

"And?" Chris pressed. "Where did they go together?"

"Ian had plans to visit with Judie Sharrow and Clarissa Allsop." Dannel brought his phone out and showed him the last message from Osian. "He texted me when they were being driven over to visit with the judge's wife. Now he's not responding."

"Why didn't he tell me before he went? He texted me a photo from the car. Not helpful to know when he's already put himself into danger." Chris held Dannel's phone in one hand while pulling his own out of his pocket. "Why don't we pay them a visit? Make sure everything is okay."

"Should I call Haider?"

"You want to call the detective inspector in charge of the Sharrow inquiry and let him know your fiancé went to interrogate a suspect and is once again potentially in a life-threatening situation?" Chris offered Dannel's phone back to him.

"He's going to be fuming no matter when we call him." Dannel had no doubt they were in for yet another row with Haider. "Better sooner rather than later."

"Osian shouldn't have gone without some sort of backup."

"He had Ian."

"Ian? Your eighty-something-year-old neighbour isn't backup. He's decorative."

"Rude. I'm telling Ian you called him decorative." Dannel couldn't help grinning despite his worry.

"Don't. He'll enjoy it," Chris groaned. He nodded to Dannel's phone. "Why don't we send DI Khan a text message? No details. Just Osian went to see Clarissa Allsop. We'll leave Judie Sharrow out of the conversation for now. He doesn't need to know how much Osian might've buggered up his investigation."

"He might've solved it." Dannel followed Chris out of the flat. They'd made a pathetic attempt of an excuse that no one believed. "Ossie might have figured out who the killer is."

"And gone with Ian to draw the killer out?" Chris commented before they stepped into the lift.

"Sounds like a genuinely shit idea when you say it out loud."

"I'm aware. Granted, I'm usually right behind you both in making these bad decisions." Chris patted him on the shoulder. "He'll be fine."

"Yes, but 'down a well' fine? Or 'run over by a motorcycle' fine? Or 'potentially murdered by a killer' fine?" Dannel forced himself to calm down. Osian had managed to escape from dangerous situations in the past, so maybe it would be okay. "Messaging Haider."

Chris grabbed his shoulder again to keep him from walking in the side of the elevator when the doors opened. "How about you wait until we're in my vehicle?"

The response from Haider was swift. He was as enraged as Dannel expected. Likely out of worry. People tended to do that, Dannel had noticed.

Emotions were odd things to decipher.

With the lack of lights and sirens, they made it to the Allsop's fancy home after the police. Chris parked in the first available spot he found. Dannel was off at a run the second the vehicle had stopped.

"Dannel?" Chris raced to catch up with him. "The police have cordoned off the area."

"Don't care." Dannel had to know what was going on. He dodged around several police officers intent on reaching either the house itself or Haider. "Oi. Let go of me."

"It's okay, Constable. Let him through." DI Powell waved him over. She nodded at Chris, but her attention stayed on Dannel. "We have a hostage situation. What can you tell us?"

"Hostage situation?" Dannel stumbled backwards, shoving Chris's hands away when he went to support him. "I'm fine. Fine. How the hell did he end up in another hostage situation?"

"Perhaps by playing detective?" DI Powell was brutally honest with him. She glanced over her shoulder when Haider joined them. "We've got Watson here. Maybe he can tell us what happened with Sherlock."

Chris placed a hand on Dannel's shoulder for a second time. "Easy. She's not being purposefully callous."

Dannel nodded sharply. He decided to speak with Haider, since DI Powell made him anxious. Words tended to fail him when his nerves began to mess with him. "I don't know much. Ossie texted me to say Ian thought they might be able to chat with Judie Sharrow and Clarissa Allsop."

"But why?" Haider asked.

"Mattie saw a woman the night of the murder. A woman in a fancy car with a chauffeur." Dannel paused to see if it sparked any recognition in Haider. "We told him to give you a call."

"Why didn't you tell Osian to give me a call?" Haider scrubbed his fingers across his face. "The butler tells us the 'lady of the house' has been out of sorts all day. He fled when he spotted her holding an antique rifle on your fiancé and Ian."

"A rifle?" Dannel didn't wait for an answer. The sound of a weapon firing had him shoving between the two detectives and racing toward the house. "Osian."

"For God's sake, someone grab him. He's unarmed." Haider bolted after him with Chris close on his heels. "Dannel. Stop! Damn it."

One of the throng of police officers managed to catch a hold of Dannel. He didn't fight against them when they did. No point in getting himself in trouble. Not now.

Dannel stared up at the fancy manor with a sense of dread. He ignored Chris's attempt at comfort. His mind froze, leaving him with just one word. "Osian."

THIRTY-ONE

OSIAN

THERE WAS SOMETHING SURREAL ABOUT BEING surrounded by opulent wealth while being threatened with death. Portraits of influential family members on the wall. Antiques everywhere to be seen. It seemed at odds with the violence being threatened.

Osian wasn't sure how to process what was happening. He had to get Ian out of the room safely. Somehow. If nothing else, he'd never forgive himself if Ian got hurt.

"Darling. Perhaps you should put the rifle down." Ian spoke as if they were nattering on about the most recent show on the West End. Not dealing with a slowly unravelling woman with an antique weapon shoved in their faces. "Dramatics are all well and good but a little beneath us."

Osian tried not to stare at Ian as if he had grown two heads. *Dramatics?* He was a better actor than they'd ever given the man credit for. *Let's keep her talking. Maybe the butler will interrupt her.* "I can't imagine how angry Edgar's betrayal must've made you. Given your husband's behaviour."

"I'm sure you can't." She sneered at him. "Be silent. I must think."

A bit late for thinking, isn't it?

The door behind her opened. The butler stepped in, saw what was happening, and bolted out of the room. *Subtle. Aren't they paid to be more professional?*

Is there a day in butler school where they cover your client creating a hostage situation in the drawing room?

Here's hoping the butler actually calls the police.

Assessing the situation, Osian didn't think Clarissa posed much of a physical threat. He could easily restrain her. The weapon was the issue.

A large, double-barrelled problem.

They needed a distraction. He caught a glimpse of Ian out of the corner of his eye. *Well, he does have a flair for the dramatic.*

Catching Ian's eye, Osian tried to subtly nod in Clarissa's direction. But, first, they had to get her talking. It might move her away from the door.

The drawing room was cluttered with antique furniture. Expensive obstacles between them and Clarissa. Osian didn't like his chances of trying to leap over a coffee table and a chaise lounge.

I am not Superman.

And my legs are definitely not long enough to leap over both at the same time.

"There's a splendid revival of *Madame Butterfly* coming next year. Have you heard?" Ian asked calmly. He slipped off the couch and got to his feet. "It's one of your favourites, is it not?"

To Osian's relief, Clarissa lowered the rifle slightly. She seemed baffled by the unflappable Ian, who continued rhapsodising about opera. He skirted around the side of the room, forcing her to turn in his direction.

Perfect.

Genius.

I'm buying him a million silk scarves.

Maybe not a million.

Standing up as quietly as possible, Osian went in the opposite direction. He had to try to approach

Clarissa from behind. If the police arrived, it would ratchet up the tension in the room.

Tense people with weapons made mistakes.

Mistakes with weapons usually meant injury or death.

Are antique weapons prone to misfiring? Note to self, learn more about guns. If I knock it out of her hands, am I running the risk of it going off?

Do rifles just go off?

I am woefully underprepared for this.

While Ian started an argument over the most superb soprano on the current opera scene, Osian attempted to creep up behind her. He was almost in reaching distance when Clarissa seemed to realize he'd moved. She spun around toward him.

Bugger.

Too late to back away now.

Diving toward her, Osian grabbed the barrel and shoved it up toward the ceiling. His momentum knocked them both off their feet, and the rifle went off. They crashed to the ground in a heap.

"I've got the rifle." Ian's steady voice shook Osian out of his daze. He glanced down to find Clarissa weeping underneath him.

Oh, for crying out loud.

Now she's emotionally overwrought?

In the distance, Osian heard a door slamming open. He vaguely made out the police calling out a warning. He motioned for Ian to place the rifle on the coffee table out of reach of Clarissa.

The last thing they needed was for the police to assume Ian had fired the shot. Osian sat up, shifting back from the almost hysterical Clarissa. He hoped the paramedics were prepared with a sedative; she was going to require one.

Footsteps clattered toward them. He heard the police shouting "clear." *I should say something. Let them know where we are.*

Why isn't my mouth working?

I'm going into shock.

That's why I'm not saying anything.

We're alive. I'm alive. Ian's alive. Clarissa's definitely going to prison.

We're okay.

"Ossie," Dannel called out to him, breaking through the clamour of other sounds.

Osian peered over the back of the couch to see Dannel barrelling into the room with Haider hot on his heels, trying to grab hold of his arm. "I'm okay."

Dannel leapt over the broken coffee table and

dropped to his knees beside him. "Not sure you'll still be okay when Haider gets to you."

"Can I have a last kiss before I die?" Osian managed to smile despite the strain of the past hour.

"Not funny, Ossie."

"Mildly funny." Osian gave a shaky chuckle while watching one of the uniformed police lift Clarissa off the ground. Haider came over to stand beside them. "She confessed to conspiring with Edgar to murder Barnaby. She claimed it was his idea to frame Wayne. She'd intended to throw her husband and his mistress under the bus."

Haider scowled down at him. "I'll be sure to ask her all about it when I get her to the station. Think you can manage to avoid getting yourselves killed in the meantime?"

Dannel nudged Osian with his shoulder. "Told you."

"I didn't ask the woman to grab her great-grand-father's rifle and shove it in my face." Osian scowled back at Haider, who remained unimpressed. "We were invited to tea. What could've possibly been more civilized? One doesn't bring a weapon to after-noon tea, does one?"

Haider reached up and very slowly ran his hands across his face. "If I count to ten in several languages, by the time I am done, will you have come up with a much better excuse for your presence at a murder suspect's home?"

Osian waited a moment, considering his options before answering truthfully. "No."

RAIN IS GOING TO BE DRIZZLING ON OUR HEADS.

May weddings were supposed to be good luck. Olivia had sworn by it. But, on the other hand, Osian felt 90 percent certain his sister had been taking the mickey.

He'd woken up to rain. Lots of rain. Typical London weather. Osian watched Dannel sleeping for a few minutes.

"Too late to murder me in my sleep because you're tired of me." Dannel flopped over on his side. He cracked one eye open, then groaned groggily. "Why are you watching me? Bit creepy."

"We're getting married." Osian hadn't expected to wake up to such an overwhelming sense of joy.

And mild terror. Not about the marriage part, but everything else. "There'll be a certificate and everything."

"I'm aware. I've read Olivia's battle plan for the day ten times already. I've got it memorised in case I forget something." Dannel dragged the duvet over his head. "Think anyone would notice if we sent body doubles to the reception?"

"Why would you want to skip the best part? The food? The cake?" Osian could still taste the various cakes they'd sampled a few weeks prior.

"Getting married to you is the best part."

"Very romantic. Sure it's not the fact that more people will be at the reception? I mean, did I mention the cake?" Osian teased. He twisted around to grab his phone when it buzzed on the nightstand. "Chris's flight landed an hour ago. He's decided to crash on Abs's couch."

"He's not sleeping on her couch." Dannel's voice was muffled by the duvet.

"Not going to think too deeply about my best friend and Chris's sleeping arrangements." Osian definitely planned to tease her about it later, though. "I wonder who's watching his sister."

After Clarissa Allsop's arrest back in November, two more conspirators, her chauffeur and a second bodyguard, had been arraigned as well. Edgar, however, had yet to be apprehended. As a result, Chris had moved to Florida; Osian knew he was deeply concerned about his sister.

The three arrested conspirators had pled guilty after months of back and forth with the detectives and prosecution. They'd been sentenced to up to fifteen years. Osian hoped the police were eventually able to bring Edgar Smith to justice as well.

Edgar had been the one to throw Wayne under the bus. To steal Wayne's tie and use his car to hide the body. So in some ways, he was responsible for what happened to Roland as well.

It had left a lasting mark on both men. Wayne had taken an extended break from his work. They'd rallied around him to attempt to lift his spirits.

Both his and Roland's.

Roland had resigned from the police. Despite being welcomed back to the force with open arms, he'd been disillusioned by the corruption leading to his suspension in the first place. He'd lost his passion for becoming a detective inspector.

After floundering for a few months, Roland had approached them with the brilliant idea to become private investigators. They'd been chatting about it over coffees at a café when Ian joined them. He'd immediately wanted in as a silent investor.

They'd gone from daydreaming about the idea to opening an office in the West End. Not the standard place for their sort of business, but Ian had gotten them a deal on the lease. He'd also managed to bring them their first case—the missing sister of one of Ian's actors.

Osian scrolled through his messages to find one from the client in question. "Dominick wants to know if we've had any luck finding his missing sister."

"Rolly had a lead from Brighton police." Dannel dragged the duvet off his head and sat up with his back against the headboard. "Thinks she might've been living rough for a few weeks. He's sent her picture to them."

"Brighton's not a bad place for a honeymoon." Osian grinned before dropping his phone on the bed. "A few days by the beach while hunting for Dom's missing sister."

"Excellent plan." Dannel stretched his arms over his head. Osian watched the movement. He never tired of enjoying watching his husband-to-be's body in motion. "How much time do we have?"

"Enough to share a shower before Princess

Olivia shows up to organise our entire day for us."
Osian had no doubt things would go smoothly. His
sister had plenty of experience wrangling children
for a living; a bunch of overgrown toddlers who
masqueraded as adults would be no problem for her.
"Let's use all the hot water."

"Or, we can *not* use all the hot water and have
time for a morning snack before your sister breaks
our door down because your idea of a quickie in the
shower turned into an hour." Dannel ignored his
pouting. "Besides, I need to go over the timeline of
the day again."

"Dannel."

"I'm fine."

"You're stressed about the day going well. It's
going to be brilliant." Osian was glad Olivia had put
her foot down with both of their mums, who'd
wanted something fancier than getting married at the
register office. He grabbed the sheet of paper off the
nightstand where he'd written everything down in a
flowchart. "Here. Peruse to your heart's content. I'll
get our suits ready."

"They're already ready. Ian had one of his
costumers get them in 'tip-top shape,' remember?"
Dannel scanned the flowchart a few times. Osian
hated how stressed this had made him. They'd done

as much as possible to alleviate the pressure. "Tip-top shape. Only Ian uses phrases like that."

Their outfits had been Ian's gift to them. Osian had almost expected something old-fashioned or overly dramatic. But, instead, their dear friend had gotten them perfectly tailored three-piece suits.

He'd also helped Olivia book Wilton's Music Hall for their reception. They might not be interested in a traditional ceremony, but cake, beer, and a party with their friends were definitely high on their list.

"Just think about the sticky toffee pudding cake."

"I had a dream about sticky toffee pudding cake." Dannel gave him a blissful smile.

"So did I." Osian's grin was decidedly naughtier than Dannel's, who gave him a knowing look. "What?"

"I don't want to know what you dreamt about, because we don't have the time to re-enact it." Dannel carefully folded the flowchart. "Can you put this in my jacket pocket for me?"

Osian shifted over on the bed. He grabbed Dannel's hand firmly. "It's just family at the register office. Small group. No strangers. It'll be quick. We just have to promise to love each other for the rest of our lives. It's going to be perfectly fine. Plus, I've helped you rehearse what we're saying."

"And there's cake."

"Which is arguably the most important part." Osian leaned in to brush their lips together. "Cake. And being legally connected to one another for life."

"But mostly the cake." Dannel snickered against his lips. "Do you ever think about what would've happened if our mums hadn't happened to move into the same building together?"

"Only in my worst nightmares." Osian didn't think he wanted to imagine a life without Dannel. It would be like a desaturated rainbow. "Oz without D?"

"Sounds dirty when you say it like that." Dannel pushed him away and got out of bed. "There isn't, really. A me without you."

We hope you've loved following Osian and Dannel's journey and their adventures. Craving more mysteries? Dahlia has a few for you to be checking out. Meet Motts and the quirky cast of characters in her world. POISONED PRIMROSE is a quintessential cosy

British mystery and an all-round fun story to throw yourself into.

You won't want to miss out on reading DEAD IN THE GARDEN, GRASMERE COTTAGE MYSTERY TRILOGY, BOOK ONE. With love, wit, and a murder to solve, life for Valor and Bishan is about to get bloomin' complicated in this sweet gay romance.

ACKNOWLEDGMENTS

A massive thank you to my brilliant betas who take my first draft and help me turn it into something legible. To Becky and Olivia, who always have faith in me. To all the fantastic people at Hot Tree. And also to my beloved hubby, who keeps me from losing my mind while I'm stressing over word counts.

And, lastly, thank you, readers, for following me on my writing journey. I hope you enjoyed *Crown Court Killer*. Oz and D have been a riot to write. I've greatly enjoyed them, and this definitely felt like their most fun and chaotic adventure to date.

ABOUT THE AUTHOR

Dahlia Donovan wrote her first romance series after a crazy dream about shifters and damsels in distress. She prefers irreverent humour and unconventional characters. An autistic and occasional hermit, her life wouldn't be complete without her husband and her massive collection of books and video games.

Join Dahlia's newsletter: HTTP://EEPURL.COM/QONOX

Dahlia would love to hear from you directly, too. Please feel free to email her at DAHLIA@DAHLIADONOVAN.COM or check out her website DAHLIADONOVAN.COM for updates.

 facebook.com/dahliadonovan

twitter.com/DahliaDonovan

instagram.com/dahliadonovanauthor

bookbub.com/authors/dahlia-donovan

ABOUT THE PUBLISHER

Hot Tree Publishing opened its doors in 2015 with an aspiration to bring quality fiction to the world of readers. With the initial focus on romance and a wide spread of romance subgenres, Hot Tree Publishing has since opened their first imprint, Tangled Tree Publishing, specializing in crime, mystery, suspense, and thriller.

Firmly seated in the industry as a leading editing provider to independent authors and small publishing houses, Hot Tree Publishing is the sister company to Hot Tree Editing, founded in 2012. Having established in-house editing and promotions, plus having a well-respected market presence, Hot Tree Publishing endeavors to be a leader in bringing quality stories to the world of readers.

Interested in discovering more amazing reads brought to you by Hot Tree Publishing? Head over to the website for information:

WWW.HOTTREEPUBLISHING.COM

facebook.com/hottreepublishing

twitter.com/hottreepubs

instagram.com/hottreepublishing

CPSIA information can be obtained
at www.ICGtesting.com
Printed in the USA
LVHW040954040522
717862LV00004B/206